FROZEN GROUND

A StormWatch Novel

DEBRA WEBB

PINK HOUSE PRESS

PINK HOUSE PRESS

Webb Works, LLC, Madison, Alabama

First Edition June 2019

Printed in the USA

DEDICATION

I want to thank the amazing line up of authors who have taken their time and talent to make this series happen. Vicki Hinze, Rita Herron, Regan Black, Peggy Webb, and Cindy Gerard, you are the best! What an amazing journey with a terrific group of powerhouse literary super heroes!

ACKNOWLEDGMENTS

I had the privilege of visiting Park County, Montana for the purpose of creating this story. What a beautiful area! I cannot tell you how amazing it was to walk the snow-covered ground Abbey walks in Frozen Ground. I stayed at the historic Murray hotel and ate at Gil's. More wonderful than anything else was the people. Kind, generous, determined people. The entire adventure was incredibly inspiring! I look forward to going back again someday.

LIVINGSTON 31 NEWS

Sunday, December 15
Park County, Montana

Camille Dutton pulled the hood of her extreme cold weather puff coat a little closer around her face. The temperature was barely holding at twenty degrees and would be dropping as the day progressed. Winter storm Holly was gearing up to wreak havoc. Camille shivered. What in the world had possessed her to move here? Livingston, Montana—Park County. Nature. Beauty. Cowboys. She exhaled a breath that fogged around her face. She'd fallen for a cowboy all right. He was the sheriff of Park County and totally unavailable except for the occasional date and doing his duty as a lawman. Garrett Gilmore was a lost cause. Oh well. This stop was only a steppingstone to a larger media market. Who knew? By spring she could be in Denver or Vegas.

"You're live in," her cameraman warned, his voice a rough rumble against the wind whipping around them, "three, two, one."

Camille fixed a grim expression on her face—not so difficult considering the worsening weather. "Brace for the worst, folks," she warned. "Winter storm Holly is bearing down on Park County. Holly has dropped enough snow across Washington and Idaho to spread a few inches over half the country. Property damage estimates are rising and, worse, the number of lives lost are mounting. This is not—I repeat, not—your typical Montana winter storm. This is the deadliest storm in nearly a century. Authorities are predicting that the Bozeman airport will be closed by early afternoon. Yellowstone's west gate as well as most other park gates on this side of Montana are being closed. Motorists are stranded all along the major interstates northwest of our viewing area. Please." Camille poured as much worry into her practiced voice as possible. "Please be careful out there. You have a few hours to gather any supplies you need and then you should stay home. Believe me when I say, Holly will be on top of us before dark and she's leaving a trail of devastation in her path. Be careful, folks. And stay tuned into Channel 31. I'll be out here on the front lines keeping you advised of what's happening. This is Camille Dutton, Channel 31 News. Back to the studio."

CHAPTER ONE

7:30 a.m.

ABBEY GRAY STOPPED at the bottom of the staircase and surveyed the living room of her childhood home. She inhaled deeply. It was almost as if she could smell her father's aftershave.

She sighed. But that was impossible. Douglas Gray had died a year ago.

Fourteen months ago, to be exact. It didn't seem possible. She'd just hit thirty and she had no family left. The image of her brother, Steven, filtered through her mind, but he had turned his back on her and what was left of their family years ago after what happened.

The darkest day of their lives.

Her father had insisted on referring to her mother's murder as that *awful day*. It was easier that way, he'd said. What he'd meant was that if they didn't mention murder, they didn't have to talk about the trial or the fact that the

1

accused was Steven—Abbey's brother, the son of the victim. There wasn't even another suspect.

No matter that she and her father had struggled mightily to get past what happened and to hold together the shattered fragments of their family, her brother adamantly refused to communicate with them in any way after the trial ended. He'd been taken away and that was the last time Abbey had seen him. As hard as she and their father had fought to find some way to verify his insistence that he was innocent, the evidence—an eyewitness for God's sake—had pointed to him. Still, Abbey and her father had stood by him, tried to talk to him, but Steven had refused. Year after year, their letters had been returned unopened. Eventually Abbey had stopped bothering; her father had as well.

Though she shouldn't, she couldn't help wondering how her brother was doing. Just before Thanksgiving last year the district attorney's office had called and conveyed the news that Steven had been released to a halfway house of sorts. The judge had been very specific with his sentencing. After his prison sentence was served, Steven would spend twelve months under close supervision, working and going to counseling, then he could move on with his life in whatever manner he chose as long as it was legal and as long as he reported monthly to his probation officer for another year.

So many times Abbey had considered going to see him despite his past refusal to see her or to read her letters much less write back to her. In the end she had decided that if he could live without her, she could live without him in her life. Particularly after he hadn't bothered coming to their father's funeral. She'd made the necessary calls and felt certain he would have been allowed leeway to attend had he chosen to do so. It wasn't like he was that far away. Hardly more than two hours.

But he hadn't come or reached out in any manner—not even a sympathy card.

Frankly, until now, that was the last time she had thought about her brother.

Their father had left everything—which was the house and a hundred acres of land in the wilds of Montana—to her. His old truck, the tractor and various other personal property. She understood her father's reasoning for the decision, but she had not agreed with it. Once the property sold, she intended to put half of the proceeds into an account for Steven. He could take it or leave it. The choice was his.

Abbey shook her head. How was it that such a happy childhood had turned into a stunning tragedy during their adolescent years?

"A dozen shrinks couldn't figure that one out," she muttered, pushing the disturbing thoughts aside.

She'd gotten in late last night. Too late to do anything but crawl into the bed she'd slept in the first eighteen years of her life. To make matters worse, she had promptly sunk into a dark, fitful sleep. She hadn't come to the family home since her father's funeral last October. He wasn't here. She really didn't want to be either. A maintenance service came once a month and took care of the place, inside and out. There was no reason for her to come...until now.

The insurance company had warned they would no longer carry a homeowner's policy on the house if it continued to be vacant. She had ninety days to sell it or there would have to be changes to how she insured the property. Since she couldn't imagine ever wanting to live here again now that her father was gone, selling was the better option.

Before she could put the place on the market, there was a good deal of work to be done. Going through a lifetime of what her parents had accumulated wouldn't be an easy feat, or a pleasant one. She would choose what she wanted to keep, and an auction company would come in and sell the rest. Sounded easy enough until she'd walked through the rooms, checking the closets and drawers. She had never really noticed the enormity of stuff her father had kept. Simple was not a word that described in any way the task ahead.

Before diving in, she needed coffee.

Unable to function without her caffeine fix, she had brought her coffeemaker and her favorite grounds. Thank goodness she had because the coffee in the cupboard was out of date—and instant.

The brew process had just finished as she walked into the kitchen. She poured a big cup and inhaled the amazing aroma. As she sipped the deliciously dark liquid, she gazed out the window over the sink. The sky had that look, the one her father always said meant snow was coming. She'd heard something on the radio those last few miles last night about a storm building up north, but she'd been too tired to pay attention. This was Montana, winter snowstorms were a part of life.

She would be stuck here for a few days in any event so a snowstorm wouldn't be such a bad thing. There was a generator. Beyond the window over the sink, her gaze roved the backyard from the house to the shed. The reassuring stack of firewood beneath the eaves of the shed would keep her comfortable for several days. The propane tank was still full. As long as the coffee held out, she would be perfectly fine.

Still, if there was a storm coming, she should likely have a look around outside now before the bad weather descended. A quick inventory of what her father kept in the shed and barn would be useful. She could take pics with her cell. Mr. Hansen, the closest neighbor, had sold the few horses and two cows her father still owned when he died. The conscientious neighbor had been so helpful, he and his wife both, over the past year. Calling Abbey and giving her updates. Mr.

Hansen—Uncle Lionel, he insisted when she was a child—came over a couple of times a week on his daily walks to check on the house.

Her parents and the Hansens had been lifelong friends.

Abbey didn't really have any true lifelong friends. She'd left Montana to go to university to pursue her love of writing. After graduation she dove straight into the publishing world. She'd worked in the business for five years, first as an editorial assistant and then as a personal assistant to the publisher. When her first completed novel was contracted by a publisher, she crossed her fingers and hoped for the best. Incredibly, eighteen months later her debut book had become a New York Times bestseller and the release date for book two had been adjusted to take advantage of the buzz. The contract offer for books three and four had allowed her to give up her day job and focus on her writing full time. When book three came out this past July and raced straight up the list to the number two spot, she knew she'd made the right decision.

Looking back, she was so grateful she'd been able to share the incredible success of her first book with her father before he was gone. He'd been so proud of her.

Currently she was in the middle of her fourth novel. Her publisher was chomping at the bit to get the next Abbey Gray thriller into bookstores. Unfortunately, Abbey was behind already and with all this to handle her deadline was looking less and less doable.

She'd brought her laptop along and hopefully she would get at least a little work done during this emotionally draining process ahead of her.

After her second cup of coffee, she pulled on her pearl white coat—her good luck coat, she called it since she had been wearing it when she got *the call* that a publisher wanted to buy her book. The matching cap and gloves were next, then her boots before heading out the back door. The crisp morning air took her breath. New York winters could be brutal, but they didn't come close to the cold in Montana. Snow from the last dumping lingered here and there. Against a shaded corner of the house and the base of trees. Beyond the yard, in the woods there would still be small drifts on the ground. Not once during her childhood could she ever recall wishing the snow away. She had loved it so much. She wasn't a kid anymore and life had shown her that all the lovely white stuff could be a real pain when there was work to be done, errands to run, appointments to keep.

Last year while preparing for her father's funeral she hadn't really done anything but shower and sleep at her childhood home. She'd felt numb and in a fog. Garrett had been a huge help. She smiled. She'd been wrong before. She definitely had at least one lifelong friend. She and Garrett Gilmore had grown up together, gone to school together in the same grade—though he was six months older. Everything in her life until she graduated high school and drove away without looking back had included Garrett.

Her first kiss. A wave of heat flushed her cheeks despite the cold. They'd lost their virginity together. She laughed out loud at the memory. After weeks of thorough and logical consideration, the event had proven an awkward ten or so minutes.

The funny thing was, they had never actually felt the urge to be boyfriend and girlfriend. Best friends was a far better description of their relationship. The kiss and the sex—both of which only happened once—were about preparing for what came next. They had mutually decided that if their first experiences were going to be embarrassing, they would rather get them over with together. No one else would ever have to know.

Thinking back to that summer before senior year, they'd

spent every possible minute together. If she was completely honest with herself, she couldn't deny there had been sparks. Feelings she hadn't experienced before. But he was Garrett— her best friend. They both had big plans. He was joining the Marines right after graduation and she was off to NYC to become a famous author.

Her career had gone pretty much as planned, but Garrett's had not. His father had nearly lost his life in a horse riding accident while moving cattle, forcing Garrett to stay home and help his mother run the ranch.

As Abbey made her way across the backyard to the barn, she realized she hadn't talked to Garrett since her father's funeral. He was the Park County sheriff now which meant he was very busy. During the past several months her life had been one frantic book tour after the other. With all the publicity events and the movie option, she had been overwhelmed. Not that she was complaining. What author wouldn't love to have all this happen, particularly this early in her career?

She entered the combination for the lock on the barn door. Mr. Hansen had suggested the keypad locks to avoid issues with keeping up with keys. A really good idea under the circumstances. Like the house, the barn was reasonably well organized. Lots of tools and the tractor. Abbey turned on the lights and photographed the items for her own inventory. There was nothing here she needed. The auction company would, of course, do an independent inventory before moving forward. The shed was much the same. More stacks of firewood inside. Yard tools. The riding mower.

She stared across the yard and into the woods that stretched beyond the cleared space around the house. Voices whispered through her mind. Her father yelling. Blood everywhere from the multiple stab wounds. Steven screaming that he didn't do it. Her mother's body lying on the frozen ground.

Abbey blocked the images and the sounds. Despite the horror of that awful day, this place was peaceful and beautiful. It was a gorgeous property. Finding a buyer shouldn't be difficult.

Before turning back to the house, she made a last minute decision to visit the family cemetery. The stroll in that direction took her alongside the year-round stream that rushed through the woods as if fleeing some unseen force. Not once in her life could she recall it ever drying up. The path turned away from the water's edge and moved toward the small cemetery. Her father's parents were buried there as were her parents. She'd never known her mother's family. That set of grandparents had passed away when Abbey was very small. Her mother's one sister lived in Europe. The two had never been close.

A picket fence in need of a coat of paint surrounded the small cemetery. Abbey sat down on the stone bench her father had added after her mother's death. He would come here and sit for long minutes each evening. Life had been extremely difficult for him after her murder. He'd lost his wife and his only son. Abbey had felt as if she'd stepped into the twilight zone. Of course, she'd heard of a child murdering a parent, but those horrible things were events that happened someplace else to someone else.

But this had happened to them. To her and her father. To their world.

She stared at the headstone her father had chosen for the two of them to share. The trees shaded the small plot of land reserved for burying their dead, ensuring that snow lingered against the headstones. As a child she remembered thinking of how cold the graves must have gotten beneath all that snow each winter. By the time her mother was buried here, she had been old enough to understand the cold no longer mattered to those who resided inside this picket fence.

What she had considered as the snow had fallen that first winter after her mother's murder, was what her brother might be feeling and thinking as he sat in his prison cell. Had he been afraid? Lonely? Sad?

Abbey had sat through every hour of the trial. She'd listened to all the testimony, the expert witnesses—all of it. Some part of her had never really believed her brother was the killer. Perhaps believe wasn't the right word. It was a sort of disconnect between what she was hearing and what her heart would allow her to absorb. Though he never said as much, she was certain her father had felt that same disconnect.

Steven could not have killed their mother.

Yet, the evidence and a single witness who had no reason to lie insisted that he had, and the jury concurred.

Enough with the trekking down memory lane. She stood and started back to the path. Another cup of coffee was in order and then she needed to get to work. The rasp of brush against brush had her stalling and turning toward the woods on her right. She listened for the crunch of footfalls on icy snow or frozen leaves. The whisper of bare limbs against bare limbs.

Nothing.

There were any number of wildlife species running around in these woods. Her scent had likely stirred one or more. The place had been vacant long enough for a sudden presence to prompt unrest. Nothing to worry about, she decided as she walked back to the house.

Inside, she peeled off the layers of protective outer wear and poured another cup of coffee, then checked her cell phone.

Maybe she should give Garrett a call. They could have lunch. Catch up. At some point during the arrangements and her father's funeral she had learned that he still wasn't married. Nearly a year later now, he certainly could be. She'd never been in a serious relationship, much less married. Focused, that had been her watch word. Get through college. Find the dream job. Write the book.

There hadn't been time for anything else.

Was the real issue time or had she still been drifting along in that personal fog? The part of her life that included intimate relationships on permanent pause? Had she ignored those needs to avoid having to deal with that *awful day*? In truth, had she or her father ever really dealt with the ramifications of such a tragic loss and the stunning violence it had included? It was far easier to immerse herself in her studies and then her work.

Now here she was, thirty, alone and suddenly uncertain about too many things.

"Why the hell are you going there?" Abbey shook her head. Being in this house had her obsessing about the past.

She picked up her notepad and focused on what she should be doing. Making a list of the items she wanted to keep and of those she felt compelled to ship to Steven. So far there was nothing penciled in under either heading.

Upstairs, she went into her father's bedroom and began sifting through decades of his and her mother's lives. The scent of mothballs stirred in the closet. The clothes were all in good condition. Those could be donated. There wasn't any jewelry other than a few inexpensive pieces that had belonged to her mother. There was a pearl necklace Abbey intended to keep. It was the one heirloom that had been handed down through her mother's family. She made a note of the item on her list but didn't find it in the jewelry box.

Considering her cramped apartment in Manhattan, she restrained her emotions and went for practical in her selections. She moved on to the en suite bath. A make-up table sat next to the pedestal sink. All these years, her father had left it exactly as it was the last time her mother had used it. The perfume she had worn, her few cosmetics, all sat exactly where she'd left them—except the lipstick she'd loved. Her father had never packed up any of her mother's things, so the two items had to be around here somewhere. Abbey opened the small center drawer to see if the lipstick or the pearls were there, but they were not. There was only a brush and a handheld mirror.

She was certain she had seen the missing items when she picked out her father's clothes for his funeral. The pearls had been lying atop the jewelry box. Had someone from the maintenance company put the necklace up somewhere?

Or taken it?

The lipstick wasn't something she would expect to be taken by anyone. More likely it had been lost at some point. She probably hadn't seen it the last time she was here. The mind sometimes filled in what one expected to see, particularly during a time of extreme stress—like her father's unexpected death.

She shook off the painful memory. Focus, she reminded herself. There was a lot to be done.

CHAPTER TWO

9:20 a.m.

STANDING in the middle of a homicide scene was the last thing Sheriff Garrett Gilmore wanted to be doing on a Sunday morning—any morning, for that matter. Yet, here he was.

Garrett surveyed the backyard where Dottie Hansen lay prone on the cold ground not a half dozen yards from her back door. Dark crimson from what appeared to be multiple stab wounds stained her ruffled pink dress. Strangely it didn't appear to have run down the sides and puddled on the snow beneath her. Maybe there was more under the body, but he'd have to wait until the coroner arrived to check it out. Her bare feet were blue, as much from the fact that blood no longer flowed freely through her veins as the freezing temperature. He shook his head. Who the hell would do something like this to a woman closer to seventy than sixty? Dottie had lived in Park County her whole life. She baked for the church fundraisers. Taught elementary school for nearly four decades before retiring.

It didn't make one lick of sense.

Two crime scene techs went through the somber steps of documenting the scene. Evidence would be collected. The coroner was on his way. Three of Garrett's deputies were searching the yard and the tree line, while two others scoured the house. So far they'd found no reason to suspect anything had been taken from inside the house—not even the cash in Mrs. Hansen's handbag was missing—which left them without a clear motive for this brutal act.

Lionel Hansen, Dottie's husband, had arrived home at seven-thirty this morning from a business trip. He'd driven all night to get here. When he'd unlocked the front door and come inside, he'd noted how cold it was. He'd walked through the living room and into the kitchen. The back door had been standing open, framing the view of his wife lying dead on the ground.

Rigor mortis had begun its slow, inevitable trek through her body. The coroner would make the final conclusion, but Garrett was guessing she'd been dead at least two or three hours when her husband arrived home. And that had been nearly two hours ago. Of course, the freezing temperature slowed everything down and made determining the exact time of death difficult. Since the victim had been home alone the night before, there was no way to determine when her attacker had arrived or when the murder had taken place by any other measure.

Front door had been locked, no windows were broken or open which suggested the intruder had entered through the back door. Yet, the back door showed no signs of forced entry. Had someone knocked and Mrs. Hansen stirred from sleep thinking it was her husband? Had grogginess prevented her from considering that her husband wouldn't have had to knock? Or had she assumed he'd forgotten or lost his key?

Garrett turned to his right-hand man, Deputy Sheriff Kyle Wagner. "I'm going to talk to Hansen again. Let me know when the coroner arrives."

"Will do," Wagner assured him as he lifted his shoulders, pushing his collar closer around his ears.

Garrett made his way into the house, through the kitchen to the living room and down the hall to the bedroom where Lionel Hansen sat on the bed he and his wife had shared for more than forty years. Garrett had wanted to ensure Mr. Hansen was away from the fray of official activities. This end of the one-story house had been thoroughly gone over already. Nothing had been found to indicate the killer had entered or searched any of the three bedrooms. Ushering the man into that area seemed the best way to keep him insulated from the horror in his backyard.

Hansen looked up as Garrett paused in the doorway. His eyes were red rimmed, his face somber. "There are people I need to call," he said wearily. "Arrangements need to be made."

The Hansens didn't have any children, but they were active in church and in the community. The couple had many friends.

"I understand and you have my word that we'll finish up here as soon as we can." Garrett sat down in the chair that flanked the bedside table. "I've asked you a lot of questions already, but there are a few more."

Hansen rubbed his forehead; his hand shook ever so slightly. "Sure, sure. Do what you have to do."

"About what time do you and your wife usually go to bed?" Garrett needed to determine if his scenario that the intruder had awakened Mrs. Hansen was feasible or if she had potentially still been up. Had she come into the living room, discovered the intruder and ran out the back door, or had she answered the door thinking it was her husband? The latter seemed the most logical since there was no sign of forced entry. No indication the lock on either door had been tampered with whatsoever.

What didn't fit was her manner of dress. She wasn't wearing a nightgown or pajamas which contradicted the scenario that she'd already gone to bed and was awakened by someone at the door. And the bed was still made. Whatever Dottie Hansen had been doing, she hadn't gone to bed before trouble appeared at her home.

"Since we both retired," Hansen said, then released a heavy sigh, "we've been staying up to watch the late news. Then we have a glass of warm milk and talk about the next day's plans, the weather." His shoulders moved up and down as if he didn't really know what else to say. "Night before last we were talking about Christmas." Liquid pooled in his eyes. "I don't know what in the world I'm going to do now."

"Eleven-thirty? Midnight?" Garrett asked gently, stirring him back to the question.

Hansen nodded. "That's about right. Since she hadn't changed into her gown, she may have fallen asleep on the sofa."

Or Mrs. Hansen may have been awake when her killer arrived. Garrett glanced at the bedside table. "Do you both have cell phones?" He opted not to use the past tense. The man was well aware his wife was dead. No need for Garrett to point out the obvious.

"She refused to bother with one. Always preferred the house phone. But I have one." He shook his head. "I called her about ten and told her I was heading home. She wanted me to wait until this morning and make the drive, but I didn't see the point in staying another night and, with the storm hot on my heels, I couldn't take the risk. I wish to God I hadn't gone at all."

Though he was retired, Lionel Hansen worked with the biggest auction house in Livingston. From time to time, he drove to another city or state and picked up a rare antique or some piece of priceless art. On occasion his wife went with him. It was too bad she hadn't gone this time.

The home's landline was in the kitchen with an extension in the bedroom. If some unidentifiable sound had awakened her, why not hide in the bedroom and call for help? The phone was right there. If the intruder had come in through the back door, why run in that direction? Whatever her intent, she hadn't been fast enough to escape her killer. As far as Garrett could tell, she had at least four stab wounds in the back. He'd noted no other visible indications of injury. The murder weapon may have been the missing knife from the block on the counter. Hansen had stated there was one missing. The killer had obviously taken the murder weapon with him...or *her*.

The concept that the manner of death was eerily similar to another one some sixteen years ago nudged him. Abbey's mom, Ellen, had been stabbed in the back. Her body had been on the ground in her own backyard as well.

Uneasiness slid through Garrett. He hated the idea that when Abbey heard this news she would be reminded of that nightmare all over again.

"She sounded fine when you spoke by phone?" he asked the older man.

Hansen nodded. "She was worried about the storm. Since I'd already set out, she wanted me to get home before it reached Park County." He exhaled another of those big, resigned breaths and scrubbed at his face. "Those damned Japanese vases are still in my truck."

"Would you like me to have one of my deputies take them to the auction house for you?"

Hansen closed his eyes and considered the question for a moment. He finally opened them once more and shook his head. "I should take them. I'll have to go to the funeral home anyway. I can't believe this. It just can't be." He lowered his head into his hands.

"When I first arrived," Garrett began, "one of the things I asked you to do is to mull over the idea of who might have wanted to hurt you or Mrs. Hansen."

The older man lifted his head and met his gaze. "The answer is easy, Garrett. No one. We don't have any enemies. We don't have a thing in this world worth killing for. A little money in the bank but nothing here at the house. We've not offended anyone or made anyone angry. It just doesn't make sense."

The answers were exactly what Garrett had expected. The Hansens were good people. Not at all the type to draw trouble. Their home was small and modest, nothing that would bait a thief.

And yet, Dottie Hansen was dead. Murdered.

"If you think of anything at all," Garrett said, "let me know. For now, we'll operate under the assumption this was a stranger passing through looking to steal money or something easily converted to cash."

Except the thirty dollars in cash remained in the victim's purse. Credit card was still there. There were no computers save the laptop Hansen had with him. The old television was not valuable enough to bother stealing. No silver or other goods readily marketable.

If Garrett set robbery aside, the manner of death spoke of something far more sinister. Revenge. The number of stab wounds suggested an emotional kill.

Hansen exhaled a big breath. "If it's okay, I'll just stay in here until your people are done. I can't bear to see...what has to be done."

"Is there anyone I can call to come pick you up? You might be more comfortable getting out of the house until we're through here."

This time he shook his head no. "I want to stay. I want to be here when they take her away."

Garrett put a hand on the man's shoulder and gave it a squeeze. "Let me know if I can get you anything at all."

He moved back into the living room and found Deputy Keith Sanders. "Keep an eye on Mr. Hansen," he said quietly. "I don't want him doing anything irrational."

"Yes, sir."

Garrett exited the house. He glanced at the sky. Judging by the way those clouds were gathering, the storm wasn't going to go around them. He was hoping the storm's path would edge past Park County but apparently that wasn't going to happen. Damned thing had played havoc in Canada yesterday. Eastern Montana was dead in its path and the timeline Channel 31 forecast was coming way too fast for comfort.

He located Prater, one of the deputies having a look around the yard. "Anything?" he asked.

Prater moved his head side to side. "Nothing, Sheriff. No tracks of any kind." He gestured to the long and narrow gravel driveway that led from the road through the woods and to this clearing where the house and barn stood. "I walked the length of the drive just to ensure whoever came last night hadn't gotten off the gravel. No luck. Didn't find any foot-prints anywhere around the house. With that recent snow melt there are plenty of soft spots, but he missed every single one."

The way the temperature was dropping anything that wasn't frozen hard would be by dark. "Make sure everything gets a second look by a fresh set of eyes. I don't want anything missed."

"Yes, sir."

The coroner's van arrived, and Garrett felt some measure of relief knowing the body would be moved soon. He hated like hell for Mr. Hansen to have to endure much more of this nightmare. It would really make life less complicated if the poor man would go to a friend's place and stay for the day—maybe a couple of days considering the storm coming. Garrett was torn between needing his input and wanting to protect the elderly man from further pain.

Doc Amos Taylor climbed out of the van on the driver's side. His assistant, Bart Henshaw, hopped out from the passenger side. While Taylor headed toward Garrett, Henshaw went to the back of the van to gather the gear they would need. Garrett had known both men since he was a kid. Henshaw had gone to school with his younger brother and Taylor was a friend of his father's. That was pretty much the way of it in this county. Everyone knew everyone else.

The rattle of the gurney being pulled from the back of the van jerked Garrett back to the here and now.

"That storm is picking up steam," Taylor said. "I've got a feeling we're going to catch hell tonight."

Garrett had that same feeling. "Keeps life interesting."

Taylor jerked his head toward the house. "So we got ourselves a murder?"

"Afraid so. Dottie Hansen."

The coroner frowned. "Damn. She's a good friend of my sister's. Is Lionel here?"

Garrett gave a nod. "He found her. Got home this morning. The back door was standing wide open and Mrs. Hansen was outside on the ground."

"It's a shame," Taylor said with a shake of his head, then, "Let's get to it."

They walked around to the back of the house together. Only yesterday the snow had been melting, the sun shining. Then the storm changed its path and the weather made an abrupt reversal. The evidence techs had finished their work around the body and had moved onto the main living areas of the house. Henshaw and the gurney rolled up behind them, the wheels crunching on the freezing ground.

Taylor crouched down and began his examination of the victim. As he moved through the steps, Garrett stood back, having another look at the scene from a different perspective. He ignored the body on the ground and visually examined the back porch. The swing was still adorned with pillows. Wood stood in a basket next to the door. No clutter. Nothing turned over or out of place.

He looked at the rug on the floor in front of the door, then traced the path to where the body lay. Other than the dead woman, there was nothing whatsoever to suggest foul play. It was just too clean.

This was the rub that chaffed at Garrett. The entire scene felt wrong. Considering that nothing was missing—at least nothing that Mr. Hansen had noticed so far beyond the potential murder weapon—this had to be personal.

If that was the case, the real question was who had a grudge against Dottie Hansen? And why didn't her husband know about it? The couple spent most of their time together. Garrett saw them around town, always together. Saw them at church together. As far as he knew, the only time they were apart was when the husband had a pick up or delivery to make. He wasn't the main driver for the auction house. More a backup driver.

Whatever happened here sometime after Hansen spoke to his wife by phone, there would be a motive. Probably a secret or two.

"Sheriff."

Garrett moved toward the coroner, crouched down next to him. "You find something?"

"Maybe." He pointed to the victim's throat which was visible now that the body had been moved onto its back. "See that fine red line there?"

"I do." Garrett studied the fine line. "It's too insignificant to be a ligature mark, wouldn't you say?"

"Not a ligature for sure, more like from a necklace or something she was wearing around her neck. Her killer may have yanked a necklace from her."

Maybe there was something missing after all.

Garrett leaned a little closer. "I think you're right. Mr. Hansen didn't mention a necklace, but I'll ask him about the possibility." Garrett frowned. "Is she wearing make-up?" Despite the lividity caused by having died lying face down and staying that way all those hours, her lips were ruby red, her cheeks almost clownish. Seemed strange for a woman with no plans other than to go to bed. He'd never seen Mrs. Hansen made up like this at any time.

"Certainly seems odd under the circumstances," Taylor commented, voicing Garrett's thoughts.

Everyone had their own little fetishes. "I'll ask Mr. Hansen if this is something she usually did."

"What really bothers me," Taylor said, his brow furrowed, "is the lack of blood. Doesn't seem like nearly enough considering the violent manner of death."

"I noticed." Garrett shrugged. "Thought maybe there was more of it under her." But there wasn't. "What's your estimate on time of death?"

"I'd say between midnight and two this morning, but it's a difficult call considering her body has been outside in these cold temps."

"Thanks." Garrett stood. "If you find anything else, I want to hear it ASAP."

"You'll know as soon as I know," Taylor assured him.

Wagner met Garrett as he rounded the front corner of the house. "Sheriff, should I take a ride over to the Gray residence? See if she heard anything? Out here along Mill Creek Road, sound carries in the dark."

His deputy was correct. The road was sparsely populated, sound would carry, particularly at night. Then Garrett frowned. "The Gray residence is unoccupied," he reminded his deputy. Abbey hadn't been home since her father died. Maybe she had someone staying in the house.

"I think she just arrived late yesterday," Wagner explained. "My wife spoke to her during her drive here."

A familiar tension rifled through Garrett. "Are you talking about Abbey Gray?"

Wagner nodded. "I figured you knew. She'll be here for a few days, maybe a couple of weeks, getting the house ready to go on the market." His forehead furrowed. "You know, my wife's a realtor."

"Abbey's selling the place?"

Again, Wagner nodded. "As soon as Abbey clears the place out, it's going on the market. I guess with her daddy gone and her living in New York, she's ready to be rid of the property. She mentioned the insurance company was giving her a hard time because the house has been empty for a while now."

The look on his deputy's face said loudly and clearly that he was surprised Garrett didn't know any of this.

"My wife said her daddy left everything to Abbey. I guess he disowned his son or something."

"Guess so," Garrett agreed. He hadn't known that part either, but he'd assumed as much.

A thought had adrenaline firing in his veins. Houses were a good distance apart in this area, but if Mrs. Hanover's killer was desperate enough, he may have sought another house to hit when he didn't find whatever he was looking for. Garrett should get over there and check on Abbey.

How the hell could she be here and not have told him?

They'd been friends since they were kids. Best friends. She'd always called him when she was in town. They'd have lunch or coffee.

"I'll take a ride over to the Gray place," Garrett said. "Make sure everything's okay over there."

"My wife spoke to her not long after we got the call," Wagner said. "She called to tell me I needed to pick up the kids after school. Before I could tell her about the murder, she mentioned speaking to Abbey. Otherwise, I would have gone by there already."

"Won't hurt to follow up," Garrett offered. "Like you said, sound carries at night. Maybe she heard something and has no idea what it was about."

Wagner gave him a nod and they both stepped aside as the gurney carrying Mrs. Hansen rolled past. Lionel Hansen appeared at the front door. He descended the few steps and followed the body of his wife away from their home for the last time.

Garrett decided he would ask Hansen about the possibility of a necklace later today. He strode to his truck and climbed in. The realization that he hadn't heard from Abbey in months—no a year plus a couple of months—suddenly dawned on him. He shouldn't have allowed this much time to go by without sending her a text message or calling.

She'd taken her father's death hard. Her grandparents had lived well into their eighties and she'd expected her healthy dad to do the same. Garrett had done all he could to help her with her father's arrangements and anything she'd needed before and after the funeral. Still, he should have followed up later.

He turned the truck around and drove toward the road.

He had idolized Abbey for as long as he could remember. Their relationship couldn't really be defined by calling it a mere friendship. There had been more, far more. But they'd always flitted just outside the boundaries of that something more. Like moths avoiding the heat of the flames. But he had always known she would be there—as his friend—no matter where she lived.

Had that changed somehow since her father's death?

Should he have done more to stay in contact? She'd been so busy with her latest book release and all the travel; he hadn't wanted to intrude. He'd kept up with her travels and all the accolades for her books. She'd made the top ten of the New York Times Best Seller List again. He'd been so proud of her.

Now there was talk of a movie. A smile tugged at his lips.

She had to be over the moon and far too busy to bother with calling a friend from her past. Maybe it was the notoriety that had changed things. She was rushing toward stardom and he was just the same old guy he'd always been.

If he was able to spend some time with her while she was here, would this be the last time? Particularly since she was selling the homeplace. She would have no reason to come back to Montana, much less Park County. The weight on his chest sank heavily against his sternum.

She'd been gone for twelve years—since the day she left for that fancy university in the Big Apple. But she'd always come back to visit. He had known she would. Wherever she went, she would come back home to see her daddy.

But now there was no longer a reason for her to come back.

He rolled to a stop at the end of the driveway that led to the Gray home. He put the truck in Park and shut off the engine. He stared at the house where he had played as a kid. They had roamed these woods. Stretched out on the floor in

25

her room and listened to music. They had even sneaked a couple of beers from her father's stash in the barn a few times. They'd laughed like idiots and danced like fools, then puked their guts out.

Abbey Gray had always been a part of his life, no matter how far apart they were geographically. No matter how their respective lives changed.

Selfishly he hadn't wanted that to change. Maybe she had met someone. Maybe she was getting married and didn't want to bother with her old ties here.

He glanced up at the ominous sky. With the murder right next door and this storm coming, this was about the worst time Abbey could have chosen to come home.

But she was and he wanted—needed—to see her.

Garrett opened the door and climbed out of his truck. His gut was tied in a thousand knots and he suddenly felt completely out of place.

Everything about this day was wrong.

CHAPTER THREE

ABBEY SAT in the middle of the floor and turned to the next page in the journal she'd used during her senior year. She'd started a new journal every year from age ten. By the time she was fourteen it was a sort of tradition. She'd been doing it since she was nine years old. When she'd started going through her bedroom, after finishing the preliminary look through in her parents' room, she decided the journals were keepers. Most other things she would donate. She'd already picked through her childhood belongings and taken what she'd wanted over the years after moving to New York.

Even at nine she had wanted to be a writer. She'd listed all sorts of story ideas in her journals over the years. One by one she flipped through the pages. Most of her first journal had been full of silly thoughts and childish ideas. Like most ten-year-old children, she had been certain she would grow up and become someone hugely important. She would travel the world and send brilliant post cards back to her family.

When she reached the final journal, her plot ideas had matured, and the silliness was gone from her ramblings. She smiled as she read the passage after she and Garrett shared their first kiss. Abbey shook her head. They had been so young and determined to burst into the future. Her heart rate picked up as she came to the day they had decided to take things a step farther. A blush crept across her face as she read the jumble of words she'd scrawled that night. They'd both been giddy and nervous. Garrett's hands had shaken as he'd touched her. But it was his eyes that she would never forget. He'd stared at her with such concern. He'd asked her over and over if she was sure...if she was okay...if he was hurting her.

Abbey closed the journal. She pushed to her feet and placed the journal with the others on the foot of her bed. She cleared her throat and swiped her hands on her jean clad hips.

"Okay," she said aloud as she gazed around the room. The journals were pretty much it.

Deep breath. That had been a long time ago. A very long time ago. Kids grew up. Dreams changed. Relationships changed.

People changed.

She walked out of the room and moved on to the third bedroom which had once been her brother's. Technically still was. Since that awful day his door was always closed but inside everything was just as it had been the day he was taken away.

The day their mother was murdered.

Abbey stood in the middle of the room and gazed around the space. Her brother had gone to college for a semester and abruptly gotten kicked out for drugs. He'd sworn he was innocent of that charge too. He'd been back home only a few weeks when their lives changed.

No point going back down that path. *Focus on the now*.

How was she supposed to decide what he might want and what to donate?

Then and there she made up her mind. She would box up everything in the room—except the furniture—and ship the boxes to him. Assuming she could find a current address. Maybe she could drop everything at the DA's office and they would get it to him. She could ask at least.

Sounded like a plan.

Time for another cup of coffee, she decided. She rubbed her arms. The cashmere sweater wasn't doing the trick of keeping her warm. Wool would have been a better choice. Maybe she would add a tee beneath the sweater. It had been a long time since she'd spent the dead of winter in Montana. Her father had generally visited her at Christmas. There was so much to do in New York around the holidays. She had wanted to share all of that with him. Though he hadn't been much of a traveler, he'd always done so whenever she asked.

He'd been a good man and a fantastic father.

Tears blurred her vision. For the first time in years she desperately wished her brother was here. She had tried so hard to hate him. To erase him from her mind after he refused to see or talk to her or their father. Part of her had never been able to accept the idea that he had murdered their mother. Whatever other problems he had, her brother had loved their mother too. But his refusal to keep contact was a different matter. Though he never spoke of it, she had watched what it did to their father.

That awful day when the police arrived and attempted to restrain Steven, he'd lost complete control. It was possible he'd gone over some edge no one else could see. Even her father had pushed for the courts to see this as a mitigating factor, but the jury had viewed things differently. Despite the dismissal from college, on that day there had been no drugs in his system, no history of mental instability. Considering the high-profile case in another state of teenage sisters killing their parents, the judge had decided to make an example of Steven, giving him a harsh sentence despite his having no history of violence and the full support of his family.

Abbey had never been able to make herself really consider the idea that he had committed the crime. Their father had even hired a retired cop friend of his to conduct a private investigation to perhaps find out what really happened. What he found confirmed what local law enforcement discovered—there was no evidence that anyone else had been at the scene other than Steven and then the witness, Dottie Hansen, who arrived merely by chance and eventually testified against him.

Her father had never spoken of that day again.

It was as if Steven no longer existed.

Shaking off the painful memories, she walked out of the room and moved toward the stairs. The upstairs was finished for the most part. She'd made her few selections for taking back to New York. Hopefully the downstairs would be easier. Once she'd made her final selections, the packing would begin. The realtor had delivered boxes for Abbey to use for her selections and for the donation items. The rest would be inventoried and prepared for sale by the auction company.

That part would make Abbey's job easier. She wouldn't have to bother with any of the sale items. She didn't even want to be here for that part. The idea was too painful.

If this morning was any indication, she might just finish more quickly than she had anticipated.

In the kitchen, she poured another cup of coffee, set a fresh pot to brew and then cradled the warm mug in her cold hands. She probably should turn on the radio and tune in to a local station to keep abreast of the storm.

Frankly, she had been enjoying the silence. There was never total silence in Manhattan. The sounds of the city proved an endless stream. The wail of sirens, the honking of horns from the impatient drivers, the moan and screech of buses, bicycles whizzing past, the constant chatter of pedestrians, the roar and rattle of the subway and the incessant hum of life.

The silence here was deafening and yet somehow calming to her soul.

A couple of thumps on the front door echoed through the house. Abbey started, almost dropped her mug of coffee. She recalled vividly the rarity of unexpected visitors while she was growing up. No one drove this far out of the way unless they confirmed you were home.

She glanced at the clock on the stove. The representative from the auction company wasn't supposed to come until Monday. Placing her mug on the counter, she moved in the direction of the bump, bump of a second round of knocking. Rather than go straight to the door, she stopped by a window and peeked out beyond the thick muslin curtains to see who was on the porch.

Garrett Gilmore.

Instantly, her heart bounced into a frantic rhythm and her face flushed with the memories of what she'd read in her journals only minutes ago.

Struggling to compose herself, she unlocked and opened the door. The rush of happiness at seeing him was the norm. She'd come back to visit her father at least once a year and she'd always spent time with Garrett. Each time was like this one, bordering on something more than mere friendship. Her heart racing, anticipation rushing through her.

She'd assumed that bond would have faded by now. Obviously, that wasn't the case at all.

"Abbey." His lips spread into a broad grin. "I didn't know you were coming."

Without hesitation he reached around her and hugged her tight. The cold emanating from his Park County Sheriff's Department coat seemed to vanish as the warmth of his embrace melted into her.

"I'm sorry. I should have called." She drew back. "Come in out of the cold."

He stepped inside and she closed the door. "Can I take your coat?"

"I could sure go for some coffee," he said as he dragged off his coat, passed it to her, then hung his black Stetson on a hook next to the door.

"I just made a pot." She wrapped her arms around his coat to restrain the impulse to hug him again. "Go on to the kitchen and make yourself at home."

"Thanks."

Taking her time, Abbey hung his coat on one of the hooks next to her own. She ordered her pulse rate to slow and the butterflies in her stomach to settle, then she drifted toward the kitchen to join him. Pausing at the door, she surveyed the man. The worn jeans, cowboy boots and chambray shirt were pure cowboy. As a kid she'd watched him learn the skills required to run a ranch. Even as his ability to calm a wild horse had blossomed, he'd sworn he was going into the Marines as soon as he graduated high school. Abbey had never believed him. His love of ranching had been far too apparent in him even as a kid. Then the choice had been taken from him. His father's injuries had changed Garrett's future.

As she entered the room, he knocked back a slug of coffee and moaned with pleasure. "You always make the best coffee. What's your secret?"

"Joe," she told him.

A frown furrowed across his brow. "Someone I know?"

She laughed and shook her head. "That's my preferred coffee brand. I brought some with me."

"Ah, I see." He lifted his cup in a kind of salute. "Good stuff, this Joe."

She moved across the room and leaned against the counter near the sink, ensuring a safe distance since her every nerve ending still jangled at seeing him. "How've you been?"

"Good. Busy. You know how it is. Tourists are always getting lost. The regulars who frequent the honkytonks like to engage in the occasional brawl. Hikers and hunters get into trouble deep in the woods." He shrugged. "Same old, same old. How about you?"

"Busy," she echoed his answer. "I've spent the better part of the past year on the road doing signings and speaking engagements." She sighed. Everything but writing. Now she was paying the price.

"Everyone's really proud of you, Abbey. You made the big time."

Abbey smiled. "I was very fortunate. Lots of writers far better than me don't get so lucky. It's a feast or famine business."

"You beat the odds." He savored more of the coffee. "I always knew you would."

He wasn't just blowing smoke. She remembered well all the times he'd told her that she was going places. He was the one person she'd dared to use as a sounding board on her story ideas. He'd always liked them and offered whatever criticism crossed his mind. A lover of books, he wasn't going to sugar coat his thoughts.

"How's your mom?" It struck her again that she no longer had any family for anyone to ask about. Strange, she hadn't realized how lonely she was until now. Maybe it was just those unexpected emotions at seeing this man. Or reading that darn journal.

"Doing really well. Mom's still bossing the wranglers around no matter that we have a ranch foreman. She still rides, believe it or not." He laughed. "She says someone has to make sure they do their jobs while I'm out catching the bad guys. In the evenings she still quilts. She swears she's starting a shop online so that when she's too old to boss everyone around, she'll have something to fill her time."

Abbey laughed. "More power to her. She's amazing." Like you, she barely bit back the words. Okay, no more reading in the journals for her.

"She's something all right," he agreed.

His mother was incredibly talented. One of her quilts was on the sofa at Abbey's apartment. She wasn't surprised at all that the woman was still running things. She always had and Garrett's father had been happy to let her. No one decorated like her either. Her home resembled something from a popular design magazine layout.

"She loves your books, by the way." He sat his empty mug aside. "In fact, she called you amazingly talented."

Abbey smiled. "Thank her for me. Her opinion means a great deal to me."

"We have to spend some time together, Abbey." His hands settled on his hips. "Last time was too hard to think of anything except your daddy. But it feels like it's been forever since we caught up."

He was right. The truth was, she wasn't sure when she would be getting back this way. Catching up would be a good thing. "Definitely," she agreed. "It's been too long."

"You know that storm will likely hit us hard later today."

"I do and I'm prepared. I have food and plenty of firewood in case the power goes out. Propane for the generator. Most important, enough wine to stay happy through the entire event."

He chuckled. "Sounds like you're good to go."

"If only I had all things packed up around here, I might actually be able to relax."

"That settles it." He gave a nod. "As soon as I'm done for the day, I'll be here to help. I'll bring the pizza."

Growing up they'd loved pizza. If they were together there was pizza involved. The memory had Abbey smiling. "I will gladly take any help I can get, and pizza would be great.

You should probably bring beer. I only have the wine I brought with me."

She had understood that this was going to be a difficult task, emotionally speaking, so she'd come prepared.

"You heard anything from your brother?"

She shook her head. "Maybe one day, but not so far."

"It's too bad. I always looked up to Steven. I never understood what went wrong."

"None of us understood. I hoped in time we'd become a family again, but I guess he still can't forgive us for not being able to save him from prison."

"Speaking of murder," Garrett said, his tone somber now.

Tension slid through her. "What's going on?"

Park County had its share of crime, but there had never been that much trouble around this area. Other than her mother's murder. It was the most heinous crime to ever happen in this part of the county. Abbey wondered, as she had hundreds of times, if her brother hadn't murdered their mother...who did? Was this unknown person still running around free? A trickle of uneasiness slid through her veins. She barely suppressed a shiver.

"Dottie Hansen was murdered last night."

A quake of shock shuddered through Abbey. She had lived in New York City for more than a decade. There were murders on a too regular basis merely because of the sheer number of people jammed into the area. But this was Park County. It was an uncommon event. The reality that it was her neighbor, a woman she had known her entire life, made the news all the sharper and more stunning.

"What happened? Is Mr. Hansen all right?" She had called the Hansens aunt and uncle when she was growing up. They had been the closest to extended family she and Steven had. The two had been particularly helpful after her mother's death.

"We're trying to piece that together," Garrett said, worry etching itself across his face. "Mr. Hansen is fine. He was out of town. Making a pickup for the auction house. He arrived home early this morning and found her."

Abbey's hand went to her mouth. Her stomach flipped and her chest tightened with disbelief. "How awful. I can't believe it."

"I'm sure sorry to have to pass along this news. I know you and your family were very close with the Hansens." A smile tugged at one corner of his mouth. "I remember she worked on the dress you wore to senior prom. You were all out of sorts because you'd ordered it, waited forever for it to arrive and then it didn't fit."

Abbey smiled too. She had forgotten all about that dress. But now that he mentioned it, she was fairly certain it was still hanging in her closet upstairs. "She was a lifesaver on more occasions than I can recall."

Dottie Hansen and Abbey's mom had been good friends. The Hansens were always coming over for dinner. Always bringing a freshly baked cake or other goodies. The best neighbors. They had no children of their own. Abbey supposed she and her brother were their surrogates. When her mother died, Dottie had cooked and cleaned and done laundry for weeks. Abbey and her father would have been lost without the couple.

"I should go over there." Abbey suddenly felt the urge to try and help as the Hansens had helped them so many times.

"We're still going through the crime scene," Garrett explained. "It'll be a while before we release the property." He plowed the fingers of one hand through his hair. "When one of my deputies mentioned that you were here, I was worried. The Hansen house is not that far from yours. The killer could have come here after..." He drew in a weary breath. "After he left their house."

"Do you have a time frame when this happened?" Abbey hadn't arrived until shortly after eleven last night.

"The coroner estimated time of death between midnight and two, but that's a rough estimate considering her body was outside in the cold."

Abbey's breath trapped in her throat. "I turned into my driveway just before midnight."

The idea that someone may have been next door murdering poor Mrs. Hansen at that same time twisted inside her.

"Did you encounter a vehicle as you were driving along Mill Creek?"

She shook her head. "It was dark as pitch. There wasn't anyone else on the road."

"Did you call and let the Hansens know you were coming?"

Another shake of her head. "I didn't. It was kind of spur of the moment. I was at a frustrating place in my work in progress and I thought the drive and the change of scenery would," she shrugged, "shake things loose."

"You drove all the way from New York?"

She laughed. "I did. I'm relatively certain I won't be doing that again."

"Still impulsive as ever, I see."

"Sometimes," she admitted.

The vague hint of a smile he'd shown as he asked the question faded and his face turned serious again. "Were you in and out of the house for a bit when you first arrived? Maybe unloading your bags?"

"I was. Yes. I got out and unlocked the door. Came in and looked around, turned the thermostat up. Then I went back out and brought in my suitcase and laptop case." She sighed. "I'm on deadline and," she held her hands up in a helpless motion, "I need to do this to get the house ready to sell."

"I understand." He searched her face a moment before asking, "You didn't hear anything in the distance? Maybe a shout or the sound of a vehicle door closing?"

Abbey concentrated hard on those few minutes of going in and out when she first arrived. "No. Nothing. It was completely quiet. The complete opposite of nights at home."

He stared at her a moment longer and she realized she had just called Manhattan home. It was, she supposed, on one level. Still, a part of her would always consider this place home.

"Have you looked around outside since you arrived?"

"I have. I checked the barn and shed. Walked around the yard and visited the family cemetery. You think the killer came through here after what he did?"

"Just trying to cover all the bases."

"What happened?" Abbey hoped the poor woman hadn't been brutalized before being murdered. No one deserved to die like that.

"She was stabbed. In the back. Repeatedly."

The news took her aback. Again, she found herself having difficulty slowing her pounding heart. So that was why he was here. This wasn't just about proximity.

As if he'd read her mind, he asked, "You're certain you haven't seen or spoken to Steven?"

And there it was. After all these years and no matter that Garrett had known Steven, her brother was suddenly a person of interest in another murder.

"I haven't seen or spoken to him." She hadn't intended for her tone to sound so curt, but the question triggered a defensive instinct she couldn't control.

"I'm not accusing him of anything, Abbey. These questions are standard procedure."

Funny. She'd just been thinking that eventually the bond between the two of them would fade. Seemed as though maybe it had. Before, he had believed Steven just as she and her father had. Had becoming a member of law enforcement changed his view?

"Why would he kill Mrs. Hansen after all this time?" Her arms had crossed over her chest in yet another display of defensiveness. She hadn't intended to let him see how this line of questioning irritated her but there it was.

"He spent a lot of years in prison primarily based on her testimony. Now he's out and no longer required to have close supervision."

Anger sparked deep inside her. "I really should get back to this." She glanced around. "Please convey my sympathies to Mr. Hansen."

Without waiting for him to answer, she turned and walked back to the front door. He followed.

"Thanks for coming by, Garrett." She managed to meet his eyes. Saw the disappointment there.

"I'll check on you later today," he offered. "I'll bring that pizza and help with the packing."

"I'm fine really."

He nodded. "All right. You know my number if you need anything."

She watched him go and promised herself she would not need anything.

Some things about this place never changed.

The newspapers, the community had been all too ready to condemn Steven. Someone was dead—murdered—and the masses wanted someone to blame. She just hadn't expected that mentality from Garrett.

Hesitation slowed her next thought, but she couldn't ignore the undeniable fact in his words. Mrs. Hansen was the one to seal Steven's fate.

If her brother wanted to hurt someone for what happened

to him, the poor woman would most likely have been the target.

Abbey closed the door and pressed her forehead there.

No, she told herself, her brother wouldn't come back here. He wouldn't kill anyone.

But what if she was wrong?

CHAPTER FOUR

ABBEY PULLED on her coat and gloves once more. She shouldn't have allowed Garrett's suggestion to get under her skin.

Still, after due consideration she had to admit he was right. Steven was a logical suspect.

But her brother wasn't a killer. She had never believed him capable of murder and she was not going to start now. Whether he ever spoke to her again was irrelevant.

Abbey closed her eyes and took a deep breath. There had been blood all around her mother's body. The butcher knife her mother had been using to slice ham from the pork shoulder on the cutting board had been rammed over and over into her back. Steven was covered in her blood. He insisted he had pulled the knife from her back and tossed it on the ground in an attempt to help her. He'd turned her over and attempted CPR.

Falling to her knees, Abbey had only been able to stare at

the scene before her. She had been in the woods on her way back from her secret place—not that the old treehouse was a secret, but she'd pretended it was. She'd heard her brother screaming and come running. Shortly after she came upon the scene, her father returned from a trip into Livingston. He had rushed around the house and snatched his wife from his son's arms. Both men had been crying and screaming.

Mrs. Hansen had been on the back porch. She'd been sitting on the steps, weeping and covered in blood from trying to help as well. She had already called the police.

Garrett was right. It was Dottie Hansen who had insisted that she'd come to the front door to borrow vanilla extract. She was baking and had run out. She'd heard Steven shouting. She'd rushed around the house just in time to watch Steven chase his mother from the house and stab her repeatedly. When he finally stopped and just sat there staring at what he'd done, Mrs. Hansen had rushed into the house and called the police. When she'd come back outside to try and help her injured friend, Steven had screamed for her to stay away. It was her testimony that confirmed the scenario the police had developed. After all, Steven's fingerprints were on the knife.

Abbey could never get right with that scenario. There had to be another explanation. Someone else had to have been in the house. Dottie Hansen couldn't have seen what she thought she saw.

Now she was dead.

For sixteen years Abbey had never swayed from her belief in her brother even when he pushed her away repeatedly. But now, the woman who cemented his fate was dead, murdered in the same manner as their mother.

Abbey blinked back the burn of tears. It was time for her to reevaluate what she had believed all these years. She walked out the back door, shuddered at the blast of cold. Her gaze went immediately to the sky. The storm wasn't going to give them a pass. It was coming. Soon.

Bracing herself against the cold, Abbey headed into the woods. Her secret place was deep in the woods where she had played as a child. A long abandoned hunting stand—the kind built into a tree—had become her private sanctuary. She'd taken all sorts of things to the treehouse. Her father had helped her. A small table with a couple of chairs. Her favorite set of pink tin dishes. A quilt her grandmother had made and a pillow.

Her boots crunched against the leaves and snow seemingly turned to glass atop the frozen ground. She had stopped going to the treehouse after the day her mother died. But the way to it through the woods was permanently etched into her memory.

When she reached the treehouse, she studied the ladder a moment before daring to climb up the rickety structure. She glanced around, didn't see any tracks in the patches of snow. Though it was more drifts here and there rather than a solid blanket, surely if someone had been lurking they would have stepped in the snow at some point.

Taking a breath, she reached for the ladder and started to climb. The boards creaked, one moved a little and she stilled, waited to see if it would hold her weight. Two more rungs upward and she could see inside the treehouse. The table and chairs her father had made for her were still there, a bit worse for the wear. There was a sleeping bag and a pillow but not the one she had put there all those years ago.

Heart pounding, Abbey climbed into the treehouse. Water bottles, some empty, were tossed about. Packaging from chips and cookies were scattered over the roughhewn wood floor. She picked up one of the chip bags and checked the expiration date. Her chest tightened. Someone had been here recently.

Abbey sifted through the items in the space. Checked beneath the sleeping bag and inside the pillow slipcover. There was nothing beyond the evidence that someone was or had been eating and sleeping here.

She closed her eyes and forced away the little voice in her head. This could not be her brother. He wasn't a killer.

A crack rent the air and Abbey instinctively drew deeper into the treehouse.

Fear seared through her veins.

She held perfectly still and waited.

The sound of frozen vegetation stirring outside raked across her senses. Someone was out there. She reached into her pocket, found it empty. She'd left her cell at the house.

She held her breath.

ABBEY WASN'T sure how long she stayed tucked into the corner behind the wobbly table and chairs she'd played with as a child. Long enough for the cold to seep deep into her bones. Finally, when the silence had gone on long enough that she worked up the nerve to peek outside, she dared to look. She saw nothing but the darkening landscape. It was midday, maybe past noon and already the gathering clouds combined with the thick pine and spruce were blocking the sunlight, making it feel like dusk.

Whoever or whatever had been out there, he, she or it was gone now. Most bears would be hibernating by this point, wouldn't they? Then she spotted the cause of part of the noise she'd heard.

The ladder she'd climbed to get into the treehouse lay on the ground.

"Damn."

The distance down to the ground was only eight or nine

feet. She could jump and maybe walk away unscathed. But if she broke a foot or leg—or worse, both—she would freeze out here in these woods before anyone found her. Particularly after she'd basically sent Garrett packing.

She shouldn't have overreacted. He was only doing his job.

"Okay, how do you make this happen?" Abbey glanced around.

There had to be another way.

She scanned as much of the woods as she could see from the door. Then she moved from one side of the treehouse to the other and stared out the open slots built in to provide a hunter with a view and a place from which to fire on all sides. Whoever had ripped the shaky ladder free of the building was, it seemed, long gone.

Still, she couldn't be certain.

She shivered. Whatever she did, she had to do it soon. The temperature was dropping far too fast for comfort.

The hunting stand was built around the tree. There were posts at each corner that held the main weight of the structure. All she needed to do was pull up a couple of floorboards near the corner or near the tree itself and she could use the tree or one of the posts to shimmy down. She'd likely still fall, but maybe not so far or as fast.

Abbey shoved the sleeping bag away and started at the corner nearest the door opening first. The gap between the floorboards was narrow in some areas but wider in others. She pushed her gloved fingers through the wide part of the gap and started to pull. She pulled with all her might. Cracking and groaning echoed in the air. But the board didn't give. She kept going from gap to gap until she found a board slightly looser than the others.

After a half a minute of rest, she started to pull again. This time the crack pierced the air and the board popped loose from the supports beneath it. The space between the supports was around a foot and a half. She could squeeze through with no trouble. All she had to do was pull up a couple more boards and drop her body through the opening and then swing her legs until she wrapped them around the nearest upright support post.

Two more boards came up fairly easily. Then, lowering her body through the opening and hanging on with her arms splayed out to the sides on the floor proved more difficult than she'd expected. She struggled to hold her weight and to swing her legs in a slight left angle.

Her elbows suddenly slipped.

She clawed at the floor to find purchase.

Heart thundering, she managed to get her fingers into a gap on either side and stop her fall.

For a moment she could only hang there and try to breathe. Again, she swung her legs. Her feet hit a post. She swung her legs once more. This time her right foot snagged the post and she managed to wrap her calf around it, then the left. With both legs locked around the post, she took another moment to relax her trembling arms.

"Almost got it," she told herself.

Finally, she dared to slip her right arm through the opening in the floor and reach for the post. With a little grunting and a lot of cursing, she managed to push her upper body forward to make the reach. Once her right hand was clasped around the post, she lowered her head and shoulders out and reached for the post with her left.

Holding her breath, she relaxed her clutch on the post and started to scoot down a couple of feet at a time. Hopefully her jeans and coat would prevent splinters from stabbing into her.

It wasn't until her feet hit the ground that she managed to take a deep breath.

Staggering to a standing position, she surveyed the woods

around her again. Still nothing. No sound. No sign of animal life or otherwise.

Then she ran. Her movements jerky at first, she didn't slow down until she reached the back door.

She propelled herself inside and then she stalled.

She hadn't locked the door.

Damn.

What if whoever removed that ladder was here?

The image of Mrs. Hansen being stabbed roared through her brain.

Where was it her father kept his shotgun? Her heart threatened to burst from her chest. She needed her cell. Needed to call Garrett.

Doing all within her power not to make a sound, she eased across the kitchen. Her phone was on the kitchen counter where she'd placed it while she donned her coat and gloves. Once she had it in her hand, she would look for her father's shotgun and then search the house.

Every second pounded in her brain as she made her way to her phone. With the device gripped firmly in her left hand, she moved toward the doorway that opened into the living room. She remembered now that her father kept his shotgun in the hall closet designed for coats that her parents had turned it into a place to store cleaning products and paper goods. There was another shotgun under the bed in his room upstairs. She held her breath as she eased across the room and into the short hall. Instinct urged her to run and forget the gun or the possibility of an intruder. Get in her SUV and drive away.

She ignored the warning voice and reached for the door-knob. Praying the closet door wouldn't creak from disuse, she turned the knob and pulled. No creak, no groan. Thank God. She reached inside, her fingers closed around the barrel of the shotgun and she drew it toward her.

It wasn't necessary to check to see if it was loaded. Her father always kept it loaded. With the butt against her shoulder and the barrel leveled in front of her, she moved back along the hall. No one popped out of a hiding place. But she checked behind the couch anyway. Living room was clear. She'd come through the kitchen without encountering trouble. If there was anyone in the house, he or she was upstairs.

She had been brought home from the hospital to this house. She knew every inch of it like the back of her hand. By the time she was thirteen and had started sneaking out of her room, she had memorized each tread that made the slightest noise under foot. Number four and then number ten.

At the second story landing, she stilled and listened. Nothing other than the wind whipping a tree limb against the window in one of the bedrooms. The first door on the right was her brother's room. She stepped inside. Clear. A quick look under the bed and in the closet confirmed the conclusion.

Next was her room, on the left. It too was clear. Nothing under the bed, no one in the closet. At the end of the hall she went through the same steps with her parents' room before backtracking to the bathroom she and her brother had shared.

There was no one in the house.

"Okay." She lowered the barrel and stamped back down the stairs.

She started to put the shotgun up but opted to hang onto it for a bit. The front door was locked. She hurried to the kitchen to lock the back door. She had considered locking it when she came inside but she'd worried she might need to run back out that way if she encountered someone in the house. There were calls she needed to make. Garrett, certainly, but not first, she decided now that she felt a little calmer. She skimmed through her contacts list and selected

Stella Ferguson, the assistant from the DA's office. Stella was retired now, but during the trial she and Abbey had grown close. Stella was the nurturing type and Abbey had desperately needed just that.

"Stella, this is Abbey Gray. I'm sorry to bother you on a Sunday, but I'm back in Montana to sell my father's house and I have a problem I'm hoping you can help me with."

"Oh my, with Holly giving us all she's got, are you all right out there in the middle of nowhere?"

"I'm good for now."

"So how can I help?" the other woman asked.

Abbey explained about the murder next door—a murder very similar to her mother's. Then she went on to detail her walk in the woods and what she found in the treehouse. Hearing the story now it sounded a bit dramatic and maybe a little like she had overreacted.

"This may be nothing," Abbey offered, "but I'm wondering if there is any way you can confirm my brother's location. I'll just feel better if I know he's where he's supposed to be." She opted not to mention that the sheriff—Garrett—had already mentioned the similarities in her mother's case and this one.

"I think I can handle that," Stella assured her.

"Great. I'll breathe easier when I'm confident this has nothing to do with him."

Stella asked how Abbey was doing, and she did the same. When the call was finished, Abbey placed the phone on the counter and decided it was time to put the shotgun away. Rather than return it to the coat closet near the front door, she placed it behind the kitchen door. The door between the kitchen and the dining room had always been left open. With it open the shotgun was well hidden. No reason for anyone to move the door.

She leaned against the counter. Though four years had

separated them, Abbey had adored Steven and he seemed to adore her as well. Once, when she was ten, she'd gone exploring in the woods and gotten lost. Usually she was better at tracking her way back, but not that time. Worse, it had been growing dark. Panic had set in. Her parents weren't home. They'd gone to Bozeman for the day. She closed her eyes and thought of the cold and the fear. She had cried for her parents. She'd been so tired, so hungry.

Steven had found her. He'd carried her all the way home. Warmed her up, fed her hot soup. Then he'd held her in his lap until their parents came home.

He'd pulled her out of a swimming hole once too. There was no denying that her every memory of him—save one—was good.

Determination hardened in her belly. Someone else must have been in the house the day their mother died. Someone Mrs. Hansen hadn't seen.

Abbey exhaled a breath. Years ago, after giving up on proving Steven innocent, her father had sat her down and told her it would be best if they put the past behind them. Steven refused to see or to speak to either of them. Her father had pleaded with her to move on with her life and not look back. He set the example, moving forward just as he'd urged her to do.

Could she have been wrong all those years with her untiring belief in her brother?

No. She couldn't have been that wrong. Her father couldn't have been that wrong.

Still, she had to make the call to the sheriff's office.

Someone had been staying in that treehouse. A place close enough to know she was back. To access the Hansen home. Her pulse rate kicked up. She had an obligation to inform Garrett in the event what she'd found had anything at all to do with his case.

CHAPTER FIVE

1:15 p.m.

GARRETT SHRUGGED off his coat and hung it on the rack in the corner of his office. It was after one and he felt as if he'd done nothing but spin his wheels this morning. They'd found not one single piece of evidence in the Hansen home to point them toward the perpetrator of Dottie Hansen's murder. They'd lifted numerous prints but so far nothing that came up with a match in the system. The murder weapon was nowhere to be found.

Garrett dropped behind his desk.

Abbey had been right next door. She could have been robbed or worse.

He rubbed his eyes and heaved a big breath. He couldn't get past the idea that she hadn't bothered to let him know she was coming. She usually did. Or maybe it had been her father who'd let him know most of the time.

He hadn't meant to stick his foot so deep into his mouth when he brought up her brother. Still, there were too many similarities in the murder scene to pretend he hadn't noticed. He'd put in a call to Ted Brisbain, the assistant deputy district attorney he worked with the most frequently. He would look into Steven's whereabouts and get back to Garrett. If Abbey's brother was where he was supposed to be, they had nothing to worry about. As much as Garrett hated the idea of hurting her in any way, he had a job to do. A woman was dead.

Like Abbey and her father, Garrett had never believed Steven guilty of his mother's murder. The idea was crazy.

But now he had a too similar murder of the eyewitness who had put him in prison, Garrett couldn't ignore the connection. He'd pulled the file on the Gray homicide case and he gone through the reports. He'd done this once before when he first became sheriff. He'd found no missteps in the investigation. The fact of the matter was, like now, they'd had nothing in the Gray homicide except that witness.

Now that witness was dead.

On one level he remained convinced that Steven was innocent, but his lawman instincts wouldn't let him ignore the possibility that he was wrong.

"Sheriff?"

Garrett looked up at his assistant who had poked her head into his office. He hoped there wasn't more bad news. "Come on in, Rayna."

She smiled and stepped inside. "I was about to go to the diner and pick up lunch. Would you like me to bring you something?"

Garrett returned her smile. Rayna was a really good assistant. She ran the office more so than he did. The former sheriff had just hired her to replace his retiring assistant the year before Garrett took over. Rayna had proved intensely loyal and incredibly diligent.

He would be lost without her.

"A sandwich would be great." He reached for his wallet.

"Leave it on my desk. I'll be back in fifteen."

He thanked her and when she'd gone, he considered how grateful he was that things had worked out even after he'd had to tell her he wasn't interested in a personal relationship. She'd been hurt but she'd taken it well. As cliché as it sounded, it wasn't her—it was him. Rayna was an attractive woman. A kind-hearted woman. Garrett had simply lost his heart long ago and, so far, he hadn't been able to get past the idea that the woman he longed to be with would never be his.

Maybe one day he'd be able to move on.

The thought had his mind going back to his meeting this morning with Abbey. She'd looked good. No surprise there. She always did. But weariness showed on her face. He felt certain this had been a difficult year for her. She and her father had been extremely close. Years ago, Douglas Gray had told Garrett that he hoped one day the two of them would stop pretending they didn't belong together.

Garrett wondered if he had ever said this to his daughter. Abbey Gray had known what she wanted to do since she was just a kid. She'd planned her escape from Montana before she was old enough to drive. She'd always said it wasn't because she didn't love the place, it was only because she had big plans.

He'd had plans as well but going off to join the Marines hadn't worked out. The truth was, he hadn't really wanted to dive into a military career. He just hadn't wanted to stay here with her gone so he'd pretended to have big plans too.

After his father's accident, he'd kept his feelings about her leaving to himself. He wouldn't have dreamed of holding her back. After all, they'd never been anything other than friends. Close friends. Best friends, but friends nonetheless. Still, they had shared intimate firsts that went well beyond friendship. If he was completely honest with himself, he would admit that he'd been in love with Abbey since he was fourteen years old.

But he'd never once ventured into that territory beyond doing so in his dreams. He would not put that burden on her back. If she had loved him in that same way it would have been different.

But she hadn't.

He still felt that familiar tug of the bond they had shared. For him, it hadn't faded at all. He would have to find a way to make it up to her for treading on her feelings where her brother was concerned. His gaze settled on the muted television hanging on the wall across the room. He kept it on the weather station most of the time. That damned storm was almost on top of them. He'd noted the crowded parking lot at the supermarket. Folks were stocking up just in case.

Abbey had said she had everything she needed. He hoped so. Around town it wasn't so difficult to get around, even after a fairly large snow. But out there on Mill Creek Road where the Grays and Hansens lived, the going got rough.

Maybe he'd call her again after the meeting with the team. This homicide case was top priority. He needed his entire focus fixed on finding the person or persons responsible for attacking and murdering an elderly woman at her own home.

Home was one place a person should feel safe.

He gathered his notes from this morning and walked out of his office. He dropped a bill on Rayna's desk to cover his lunch as well as hers and headed to the conference room. This already long day was only going to get longer.

DEPUTY SHERIFF KYLE WAGNER and Deputy Chad Sanders waited in the conference room. Reports and photos were spread across the table.

"We have anything back from the coroner yet?" It was early. Garrett knew this but he could hope.

"Nothing yet," Wagner said, glancing up from the report he was reviewing. "I stopped by the morgue on the way back. He's started a preliminary examination already. He hopes to have something in a couple of hours, but it may be tomorrow. He said he'd do the best he could."

"I'll damned sure owe him one if he can get this one done ASAP." Garrett pulled out a chair and dropped into it. "Where's Mr. Hansen?"

"He insisted on staying at the house and cleaning up after we finished. He didn't want anyone else to do it."

Garrett exhaled a weary breath. "Hardheaded old man. He should have gone to a friend's house or over to his sister's in Belgrade and let a professional cleaning service take care of things." There really wasn't so much to clean up and even that was outside. But dealing with the blood—even only a small amount—of a lost loved one would be difficult.

When folks reached a certain age, there was no changing their minds once they were made up. Especially after such a traumatic and tragic event. The man's wife of nearly fifty years had been murdered. He couldn't be expected to make rational decisions.

"How are we coming on the search around the outer perimeter of the crime scene?"

"No vehicle tracks. No foot prints. We got nothing, Sheriff," Sanders chimed in. "We've checked with the entire list of friends Mr. Hansen provided—it wasn't that long—and no one spoke to the victim yesterday or last night."

Garrett glanced at Wagner. He picked it up from there. "A bulletin—a plea for information—went out on all the local news stations as well as radio stations. We're running the MO through the data bases. Nothing so far other than the similarities between Mrs. Hansen's murder and Mrs. Gray's all those years ago."

"I have a call into Brisbain. He's getting me a location on Steven Gray."

Both men nodded. That scenario didn't sit right with Garrett, but he couldn't pretend it wasn't a logical possibility.

"Did you confirm Hansen's alibi?" Garret had known Lionel Hanson as long as he'd known anyone in this town, which meant his whole life and he hated like hell to treat him like a person of interest in this case, but it was standard operating procedure. He was the husband of the victim; he had to be ruled out.

"I did," Wagner confirmed. "He picked up the package in Spokane at five p.m. on Saturday. Slept for a few hours at a motel," Wagner glanced at him. "I confirmed. He checked out of the motel and headed home, just as he stated. The mileage on the truck verifies he drove from Livingston to Spokane and back. No deviations or additional mileage unaccounted for."

Which meant Hansen couldn't have come back and killed his wife. Not that Garrett had actually believed he had. He couldn't fathom a motive. But that didn't mean one didn't exist. Until he discovered one, he had every intention of considering the man innocent.

"So what we have," Garrett offered, "is nothing except a victim stabbed in the back, in the middle of the night, outside her own home."

He still needed to ask Hansen about the lipstick and the necklace. That odd little fact nagged at him. Seemed a bit odd for the middle of the night.

"I checked to see if there have been any break-ins in the surrounding areas and found nothing so far," Sanders put in.

Garrett scrubbed at his jaw. He hadn't taken the time to shave this morning. The call had come in and he'd hit the road. "Hopefully, Taylor will find something to point us in the right direction. Did Hansen say his wife wore a necklace? If there was one and it's missing, we need a description."

Wagner said, "He doesn't think she has one. He said his wife rarely wore jewelry. Or makeup."

Garrett would give Hansen a few more hours to pull himself together and do what he had to do and then he'd question him again. They were missing something. There was no other explanation.

Rayna showed up with sandwiches. Garrett and the two deputies ate in silence as they reviewed the notes and reports from this morning. Rayna ate in her office, fielding calls. Word had spread about the murder and people were worried.

"Ms. Gray didn't see or hear anything?" Wagner asked.

"She didn't," Garrett confirmed.

"My wife said she's already had several inquiries about the Gray property. It may sell quickly."

The murder next door notwithstanding, Garrett didn't mention.

"Funny thing," Wagner went on, "Mr. Hansen talked to my wife about the property. You know," he shrugged, "asking price and that sort of thing."

"Maybe he wants to expand," Garrett said. Didn't make a lot of sense at his age but stranger things happened.

"I can't see any way the sale of that property would have any impact on the case," Sanders commented.

"Probably not," Wagner said. "If anything, it might make the property more marketable. Some folks are just downright bizarre. Near identical murders, sixteen years apart, right next door to each other."

Garrett couldn't deny that allegation. There were those who loved mysteries and got some serious gratification from being near where that sort of event occurred.

"Give me an update on the storm." Garrett had noted the signs that serious trouble was in the air. He could hope, but he was reasonably sure they wouldn't dodge the bullet on this one. Holly wasn't going to be the typical winter storm.

"We've got until dark, tops," Wagner said. "The local channels are pushing the warnings. Holly's coming. And she's coming hard."

Damn. Garrett could do without that storm for the next few days. No one liked a fresh snowfall more than him. But there were times when it presented way too many complications. Like now, when he had a murder investigation in front of him. Worse, Holly wasn't just going to drop a fresh blanket of snow. The projected precipitation amounts coming in this blizzard were best measured in feet rather than inches.

"Let's do what we can," Garrett said, "before the storm hits." His cell vibrated against his side. "Keep me up to speed on anything you find."

The deputies headed out and Garrett answered his cell without checking the screen. "Gilmore."

"Hey, Garrett, this is Ted."

Brisbane. Garrett's pulse tripped into a faster rhythm. "I hope you called to tell me Gray is right where he's supposed to be and that you spoke to him personally."

"I wish that were the case," he said with a sigh. "I spoke to his employer. Gray was at work on Friday. He was scheduled to be off yesterday, but he was supposed to come to work today and he didn't show. His employer gave me his address and cell number. I couldn't reach him on his cell, so I called a detective friend over in Billings and asked him to check the duplex where the guy lives. No answer at the door. Yesterday's mail was still in the box and the car registered to him wasn't in the driveway."

Garrett swore silently. This was not good. Before he could ask, Brisbain went on, "I even called the hospitals to see if he'd had an accident or something. No one by that name has been admitted in the past forty-eight hours. This, of course, doesn't mean he drove to Livingston and committed your murder, but it's sure one hell of a coincidence."

Garrett got the details on the Steven's car, just in case. "Thanks, Ted. I appreciate you looking into the situation for me."

The call ended and Garrett exhaled a big breath. He needed to talk to Abbey whether or not she wanted to hear what he had to say. He glanced at his phone, shook his head. He needed to do this in person.

"Sheriff."

Garrett glanced up at his assistant. "Thanks again for the lunch."

She blushed. "Thank you."

He smiled. "I was about to head out. Did you need something?"

"Scott Pearson over at the market called and said he was supposed to make a delivery to the Gray address, but he wasn't sure if you still had the road cordoned off on that end."

"It's clear," he said, then hesitated. "I have to drive out and talk to Abbey. Let Scott know I'll pick up the delivery and take it out to her."

Rayna smiled. "I'll tell him."

"And, Rayna. Go home early. That storm is coming and it's looking worse all the time."

She nodded. "You be careful, too, Sheriff."

Garrett checked the messages on his desk. Nothing that couldn't wait. He locked up and headed to Scott's Market.

Scott, the owner, waited for Garrett at the front entrance. He'd rolled a loaded cart into the lot by the time Garrett had braked to a stop in a parking slot. He climbed out of his truck and opened the back door of the crew cab.

"Looks like that storm is going to be just as bad as they're saying," Scott offered as he passed the first of three bags to Garrett.

"I've got four of my deputies going from door to door to check on the older residents," Garrett said. "Livingston's got a half dozen of their own doing the same. We want to be sure everyone knows we're in for a bad one."

Scott passed him another bag. "I had to call in my entire crew. A lot of those folks have called in requesting deliveries."

The market didn't make deliveries all the time—unless it was to the elderly or disabled—but in this kind of weather Scott and his crew did all within their power to ensure those in the community who needed extra help had it. Like his daddy before him, Scott cared deeply about this community. He was passing that same tradition onto his own son. The kid had just started his first semester of college and still he was here working every weekend and break.

"Glad to hear it." Garrett accepted the last of the three bags. "Let me know if you run into any trouble or see anything out of place."

"You know I will." The older man shook his head. "Sure is a shame about Mrs. Hansen. You got any leads yet?"

Garrett wished he did. "Not yet. But we're doing all we can."

"I watched the breaking news report. You think whoever did this is still hanging around?"

"Can't be sure but we don't want to take any chances. An appeal to the community for help and a warning to take special care was in order."

"Stuff like this just doesn't happen around here." Scott seemed to catch himself on the last. "Not for a long time anyway."

Garrett nodded. "Yeah, it's been a long while." He closed the truck door. "Thanks, Scott. I'll get the order out to Ms. Gray right away."

"I heard she was back to sell the family place."

"It's time I guess." Garrett couldn't blame her, even if it felt wrong.

"You know, I read a couple of those books she wrote. Pretty scary stuff. Makes you wonder how a person—even one as nice as Abbey—could come up with something like that."

"It's fiction," Garrett reminded him. "After what she went through with her mother's murder, it's not surprising she understands that kind of darkness."

"Guess not," Scott agreed.

Garrett bit back a flare of anger. People would talk and come up with all sorts of scenarios to explain away the gruesome murder of a local. But Abbey Gray was the last person anyone should be considering. She would never hurt a soul.

At some point before this day ended, he would have no choice but to warn the community to be on the lookout for her brother Steven. But he wasn't doing that until he had some sort of proof the man had headed this way. He wasn't bringing that kind of scrutiny down on Abbey unless he had no choice. He had, however, decided to issue a BOLO for his car. He'd deal with that if the vehicle was located in his jurisdiction.

As he climbed back into his truck, his cell vibrated again. He answered without taking the time to check the screen. "Gilmore."

"Garrett, this is Abbey."

She sounded strange. Unsettled or worried. Maybe both. "Hey. Everything okay?"

"Probably. I'm not sure. Maybe it's nothing, but with what happened next door I don't want to be too cavalier."

Tension rolled through him. "I'm listening."

"I did some walking around the property a little while ago. I ended up at that old tree stand that we turned into a treehouse."

A smile tugged at his lips. "I remember the place."

"As I said, maybe it's nothing, but it appears someone has been staying there. I found empty water bottles and snack packaging."

His tension moved to the next level. "I'll be right there."

CHAPTER SIX

STEVEN.

Abbey hugged her arms around herself. Her thoughts kept going back to her brother. She didn't want to believe the worst. And it made no sense. Why would Steven do any of this after all these years? He'd served his time. From all accounts, he had played by the rules during his incarceration and then for more than a year after his release, and suddenly he does this?

Where was the logic?

But then, Abbey didn't know Steven, the man. She only knew the teenager he'd been more than fifteen years ago. After all those years in prison, he probably was nothing like the boy she had known growing up. They had explored these woods, climbed to the tops of every ridge in sight on those mountains that surrounded this valley. He'd always protected her from danger.

If bitterness and hatred had consumed the good in him and revenge had burrowed into his soul, why now? What was the relevance of the timing? Why kill the woman who testified against him *after* he paid his debt to society? Why risk ending up back in prison? The only reasonable explanation was that maybe there was an undiagnosed mental illness and it had worsened. Now that he was mostly unsupervised had he even seen a doctor much less a counselor?

Once he was imprisoned, Steven had ensured that she and her father were no longer authorized to be made aware of or to question anything about him. If he had died in prison they wouldn't have been notified. Their only link to Steven all these years had been the district attorney's office. But even the DA was not allowed to pass along any news of his physical or mental health. As the victim's family, they were notified of any change to his status as related only to his incarceration.

Abbey walked to the front window and checked to see if Garrett had arrived. She felt guilty now for waiting to call him until after she heard back from Stella. But she'd hoped to have some confirmation of her brother's whereabouts. Stella hadn't been able to reach him or his parole officer. It was Sunday and only days before Christmas.

Stella had agreed that her inability to reach him did not mean he was back in Park County and certainly not that he had murdered anyone.

Still, Abbey's hopes had plummeted with the news.

The snow had started to fall in earnest now. Channel 31 had already warned that Park County was in for more snow than anyone around here had seen in years. The sky and the strange shift in the wind warned that Holly was close.

Abbey wasn't really worried. She was prepared well enough to get through the storm. But what about whoever had stayed in that treehouse? What if that person was her brother? He could freeze to death in the coming storm.

Worry washed over her. She shouldn't be concerned about his wellbeing. He'd certainly made it more than clear that he wanted nothing to do with his family. Unless he wanted her dead. She blinked away the thought. She had no reason to suspect he felt that way. He'd never said anything of the sort during the trial. He'd insisted he was innocent, and Abbey and her father had believed him.

It made no sense. If anything, Steven had been closer to their mother than Abbey. She had always been a daddy's girl. More of a tomboy. She exhaled a big breath. Felt that overwhelming sense of loneliness again. When her mother and Steven were gone, she'd still had her father. Now there was no one but her. Once this place was sold, there truly wouldn't be a reason to come back to Park County.

As if the thought had summoned him, Garrett Gilmore rolled up the driveway in his big black Park County Sheriff's truck. Her heart twisted the slightest bit. There were still people here who were like family. Garrett was one of them.

This place would always be home whether or not she ever came back.

She watched as he climbed out of the truck and then held his hat in place as he bounded across the yard and onto the porch. He stamped the snow from his boots and knocked.

Despite the current circumstances, a smile tugged at her lips as she opened the door. "It's getting pretty bad out there."

He stepped inside and she immediately closed the door to keep out the freezing air that whipped the snow around, sending it swirling through the door. "And it's only going to get worse," he warned.

He shrugged out of his heavy coat. She took it and his hat. "There's fresh coffee in the kitchen."

"Sounds good. It's cold as hell out there."

In this part of the country, hot, fresh coffee was a mainstay during long winter months. She hung his jacket on the rack next to the door, only then noticing that her father's was still there. When she'd placed Garrett's hat on the shelf above the rack, her fingers trailed down her father's *everyday* coat. It was the one he'd worn when working in the barn or puttering around the yard when there was a chill in the air. Whenever he went into town or to church, he had his *Sunday* coat. How in the world would she part with this piece of him?

When she pushed the painful memory away and turned around, Garrett walked back into the room carrying two mugs of coffee. He passed the one she'd left by the coffeepot —the one she'd been using—to her, brimming with hot, steaming coffee.

"Thanks." She was running on caffeine overload at this point but what was one more cup?

An awkward moment passed with them both simply standing there. "Please, sit down." She settled into the side chair that had been her mother's favorite.

She suddenly realized that her life growing up in this house had been so very different than her life in the city in far more ways than the landscape and the way of life. New York apartments were notoriously small, ensuring she kept her decorating and furnishing on the sparse side. She'd filled the small spaces with modern, stylish furnishings. Here, her parents still had the same stoneware and cast-iron pots and pans from when they first married. The furnishings were the same ones from her childhood. The sofa and chairs were a little worse for the wear but still perfectly serviceable and reasonably charming.

And more than comfortable. Her body fit into this old chair as if it had been built for her. More likely the cushions had molded to her frame over the years. Her mother had been the same size as she was now.

"I'd like to have a look around the treehouse," he said, dragging her back to the present with his deep voice.

The sound warmed her. She would have liked to chalk up the flush of warmth to the coffee only she hadn't so much as taken a sip. No, it was him. He'd always made her feel safe and cared for. Warm. "Of course. I'll feel far more at ease when you've had a look around. I wouldn't actually be concerned if the dates on the snack packaging hadn't been so recent. With the murder..." She shrugged. "I had to tell you about it."

"It's possible a hunter has used the treehouse recently, but I don't think your father had any arrangements with anyone as far as hunting goes which means whoever was there, was trespassing."

Abbey had considered this as well. "If it turns out to be a hunter, I'm okay with that. I'm just hoping it has nothing to do with Mrs. Hansen's murder."

"The location puts it about halfway between your place and theirs."

The concern on his face told her this was the part that bothered him. Since the last snow had melted for the most part, finding tracks wasn't likely. That would change, however, with the way the white stuff was coming down now. If the trespasser dared to show up again, he wouldn't be able to avoid leaving behind tracks.

"If he shows up again, we'll know," she said, voicing her thought.

He nodded, chugged more of his coffee. When he stared into the cup once more, he said, "I was thinking it might be better if you came into town and stayed for a few days. Until we get a handle on the Hansen murder."

A chill trickled through her. The idea had crossed her mind. She wasn't foolish enough not to see the danger. "I don't have a lot of time, Garrett. There's so much here to do and I have a deadline looming. I really need to stay and get this packing done."

Falling any farther behind on her deadline would be a serious problem. She was genuinely concerned about her ability to meet the date that had been pushed out once already—at her request. She did not want to ask for another extension. Particularly not with contract negotiations coming up after this book was turned in and accepted.

He set his mug on the table that fronted the sofa. "I spoke to Ted Brisbain. He's a Park County DDA I've worked with on a number of cases. At my request, he called a friend of his, a detective who lives in Billings. He dropped by the duplex where Steven lives. Didn't appear he'd been there in a couple of days. Brisbain went to his employer then. Steven worked on Friday, but no one has seen him since. When he didn't show this morning, his boss attempted to reach him by phone and got nothing."

This was the news Abbey had hoped not to hear. Part of her had recognized that Steven's involvement was a possibility—one she couldn't so easily dismiss under the eerie circumstances. But she had hoped that wouldn't be the case.

"So he could be anywhere?"

Garrett nodded. Then he closed his eyes and shook his head. When he opened them once more, he said, "I hated to pass this news along to you, but this isn't the time to play loose with the variables. I can't fathom why Steven would come back and do something like this, but it's a risk I can't take. I have to consider him a suspect until he's been located and cleared."

"I wouldn't expect anything less," she agreed, in hopes of providing some measure of relief for the guilt he obviously felt at coming to the conclusion. "I'm sorry about the way I overreacted when you were here earlier. This is an emotional time for me."

"I understand. We've been friends far too long to doubt each other's motives."

He had her there.

"Under the circumstances," he went on, "I'm hoping you'll change your mind about staying in town for a few days.

You're welcome at my home anytime. You know this." He chuckled. "Mom might ask you a million questions about the next book. She can't wait to get her hands on it."

"The next book is one of my problems," Abbey admitted on a weary sigh. "I'm behind already. I can't afford not to stay on track at this point." She shrugged. "With everything I need to do to prepare the house for going on the market, I feel like I'm drowning." She pressed his gaze with her own. "I'll be okay, really. I have Dad's shotgun. Scott's Market will be delivering my order any time now. I'm all set."

"Your order. I almost forgot." He stood. "I stopped by and picked it up since I was headed this way." At her confused expression, he explained, "Scott called to confirm whether the road was open after we'd blocked it off this morning."

Abbey sat her untouched coffee on the table next to her chair and pushed to her feet. "Makes sense. I can help you bring everything in."

He held up a hand. "I've got it. No need for both of us to go out there."

Before she could argue he'd hurried out the door without his coat or his hat. By the time she'd reached the door he had returned with two bags. She followed him to the kitchen where he deposited his haul onto the counter and went back for the third. Abbey stared at the damp-with-snow paper bags for a moment before she had the presence of mind to start putting things away.

If Steven was here, had he come to see her? If so, why hide? She hadn't written him since their father died, but even then she had told him she loved him and would like to see him. It was possible he had heard she intended to sell the place and decided to come and then lost his nerve when it came to facing her.

But where would he have parked? Why hide in the treehouse when he could have knocked on the door? This was his childhood home the same as it was Abbey's. Why not call?

Unless he was guilty of something.

Hurt and disappointment rolled through her. She did not want to think the worst, but how could she pretend it wasn't a distinct possibility? She wasn't that naïve.

The sound of Garrett returning with the final bag spurred her back into action. She placed the milk in the fridge and reached for the eggs to do the same.

He placed the final bag on the counter and lingered a few feet away for a moment before saying, "I want to have that look around now. Lock the door behind me. We'll figure out what's next when I return."

Rather than argue, she nodded and followed him to the door. He pulled on his coat and hat, and she watched him cross the porch and descend the steps. When he'd disappeared around the corner of the house, she closed the door and locked it. Part of her wanted to pull on her boots and coat and go with him.

Instead, she rounded up her father's shotgun and stood vigil at the back door. She watched beyond the glass as Garrett disappeared into the woods. He was right. The snow was coming down really hard now and the wind whipped madly. But the weather didn't scare her. What terrified her was what blew in with this damned storm.

Murder.

A woman was dead.

A woman she had known her entire life.

A woman her brother had every reason to want dead.

CHAPTER SEVEN

THE GROUND WAS COVERED NOW. Even this deep in the woods with the canopy of trees overhead, there was already an inch or more blanketing every horizontal surface.

Garrett pulled the brim of his hat down lower to prevent the snow from flying against his face. The cold wind blew just hard enough to be annoying. The temperature had fallen dramatically in the short time since he arrived at Abbey's. By tomorrow morning they would be lucky to hover barely above single digits.

The timing of this storm could not be worse. He had a murderer to find. On top of that, he needed to ensure Hansen and Abbey remained safe. At this point they were the most likely targets in the killer's crosshairs—assuming he was even still around. If the murder had been a random attempted robbery by a stranger just passing through, then he was likely long gone. But if Mrs. Hansen's murder was about the past, then he was in all probability still here. Worse, if the latter was the case, there was a good possibility the killer was Abbey's brother.

Like Abbey, Garrett hadn't seen Steven since the trial.

Back then, at fifteen, Garrett wasn't the slightest bit interested in law enforcement as a career. Patrick Fielding had been the sheriff in Park County for as long as Garrett could remember. After his father's accident, he'd spent a couple of years just taking care of the ranch. Eventually he'd needed more. It was Fielding who'd talked him into becoming a deputy. Abbey's rush off to New York to follow her dream had left him feeling unmoored. His family had needed him more than ever. He couldn't exactly pick up and leave—no matter that his mother had attempted to talk him into just that. Even then, she had understood how he felt about Abbey.

But he'd stayed. Three years after he'd joined the department, his father had died. Abbey had come home for the funeral. She and her father had been there for Garrett and his mother. But afterward she'd gone back to New York. He'd watched from afar as Abbey's dream came true. He'd been happy for her, though he'd missed her. He'd learned to settle for her rare visits. It was difficult to believe more than a decade had passed. Closer to thirty-one than thirty, it wasn't like there wasn't plenty of time for him to build a future with someone. His dad hadn't married his mother until he was thirty-two. No need to rush into a lifelong commitment.

Still, the rest of his and Abbey's graduating class were happily settled in relationships. Most had kids.

As far as he knew, Abbey was like him and hadn't had a serious relationship.

He'd often wondered if that meant she felt the same as he did—that the one for him was unreachable.

Probably not. Abbey loved her work and her life. It was doubtful she even thought of him other than when she came home for the occasional visit. He was glad she was happy. Even if he was a little jealous.

The treehouse, former hunting stand, came into view in the distance. Garrett pushed forward, pressing into the wind.

He wanted to have a look then get back to the house to try and somehow convince Abbey to be reasonable. Staying out in this remote area with Holly descending and a murderer on the loose was irrational.

The fallen ladder was mostly covered with snow as he approached. Grateful for his thick gloves, Garrett picked it up and leaned it against the base of the treehouse. The splintering of the wood at the top told him someone had knocked it loose. It might not have taken much but the damage hadn't happened without a little help from some sort of outside force.

One more knot tied in his gut. Someone had been out here with her—too damned close.

Garrett shook off the troubling thought as he again scanned the freshly fallen snow. Cold leached beneath his coat and through his flannel lined jeans. No tracks beyond his own. Confident the ladder was steady enough, he climbed into the treehouse. He saw the boards she had pulled up to get down without jumping. He noted the table and chairs, the sleeping bag and pillow, and shifted his attention to the discarded food and drink packaging. The chip bags confirmed Abbey's belief that the visitor had been staying in the treehouse recently. Garrett took his time, sifted through the bags and bottles, checked under the sleeping bag and pillow. Nothing stashed under the tabletop or the seat of the chairs.

He stood then and surveyed the primitive wood walls and ceiling. No markings beyond the ones he and Abbey had made as kids. They'd each carved their names into the wood. He removed his glove and traced his fingers over the groves that spelled out her name. He'd never imagined a life that didn't include her.

His mother had told him more than once that he should share his true feelings with Abbey, but his ego wouldn't let him. He'd come close a couple of times, but he'd backed out at the last minute.

"Sad, really sad," he muttered as he tugged his glove back on.

There wasn't anything in the treehouse that gave him pause beyond the discarded packaging and sleeping bag. No question someone had been here. The only question that mattered was did that person have anything to do with Mrs. Hansen's murder. He pulled an evidence bag from his coat. He'd tucked a couple into his pocket this morning while going through the Hansen scene. He selected a water bottle and a chip bag, placed both into the evidence bag.

After one final look around, he climbed down the ladder and headed back toward the house. The wind was at his back this time, making the going somewhat easier. With the white stuff whipping around him, the tracks he'd made coming this way were already mostly covered and nearly invisible. He stopped from time to time to survey the area around him. He didn't spot any other tracks. Not that he really expected to in light of the weather, but he had to be certain. When the barn came into view, he broke through the tree line, moving faster toward the back door of Abbey's house.

She was watching for him and opened the back door as soon as he was on the porch. He stamped the snow from his boots and hurried inside. The warmth immediately enveloped him.

"I built a fire," she said, "you should warm up before you head back into town."

He recognized the offer for what it was: a reiteration that she had no intention of leaving.

In the living room, he tugged off his gloves, tossed them on the hearth and held his open palms toward the flames. The heat seared through his freezing hands. "I don't believe leaving you out here alone is a good idea."

She gestured to the shotgun propped next to her chair. "I'll be fine. I'm certain you remember that my father made sure I was proficient with that thing before I was twelve."

"You didn't sound fine when you called to tell me about what you'd found in the treehouse." This was not a point she would appreciate him making but there was no help for it. She needed to understand this was not the time for misplaced bravado. That treehouse was less than half a mile from her back door. Someone had been holed up there very recently. The idea that a murder in the area had occurred just last night made what could simply be a coincidence something far more.

"I was shaken, yes," she admitted, her shoulders squaring with the reluctant confession. "But whoever has been staying out there is long gone, I'm certain. Who in his right mind would wander in the woods with a storm like Holly flexing her muscles?"

Her conclusion held some merit. "What about around your barn? The woodshed? You're certain there's no one been lurking around there?"

"I was out there this morning. I didn't see anyone or anything that would suggest so. But you're welcome to look if you feel it's necessary."

If he'd thought she might have mellowed with age, he'd been wrong. Abbey Gray was still just as headstrong and independent as ever.

"I'll post a deputy to keep an eye on things." The boots on the ground search for Dottie Hansen's killer would end at dark so he'd certainly have an extra deputy to assign to the detail, but he'd feel better if she was at the ranch...*with him*.

"Do not waste resources on me, Garrett Gilmore," she argued with an adamant shake of her head. "I can take care of myself. I'm not going out that door and I have no intention of allowing anyone to come through it. You should focus on your investigation, *Sheriff*."

Well, that was plain enough. The determination on her face and the crossing of her arms over her breasts underscored her words. He couldn't exactly make her go. With a sigh, he reached for his gloves and tugged them on. "Since I can't force you without arresting you, I suppose I'll be on my way."

"I don't mean to sound ungrateful." She mustered an apologetic smile. "Like I said, I have so much to do and, obviously, you have your hands full."

Before his brain could override the decision, he'd walked over to her and pulled her into a hug. The feel of her body next to his almost undid him. "I just want you safe."

She hugged him back. "I appreciate that." She drew away, searched his eyes. "If Steven shows up, I'm not afraid of him. I refuse to believe he would kill anyone, much less our mother or Mrs. Hansen. Wherever he is, he has some reason that doesn't include revenge or guilt or *murder*. I'm certain of it."

Garrett wanted to be certain, but his lawman instincts wouldn't allow him to go quite that far. "Just be careful. Think long and hard before you let him in—if he shows up at your door."

"I will. Now go," she nodded toward the door, "before the roads get any worse."

She followed him to the door and when he walked out she closed and locked it behind him. He glanced back at her one last time before hurrying through the snow and wind to climb into his truck. She watched from the window as he backed up and turned to drive away. He waved again, and she waved back.

Part of him resisted the idea of leaving, but she was right. He had a murder to solve.

When he reached the end of her long, snaking drive, he made a right onto Mill Creek and headed back to town. The Hansen place was in the opposite direction, but only a mile at most. Most of the road that was Mill Creek was dirt and gravel. A mile or so before intersecting with Highway 89, the dirt and gravel gave way to pavement. But here, there was no pavement and no true shoulder. Passing another vehicle or getting off the road wasn't a simple matter, particularly in this weather. With the storm coming, staying off the road once darkness fell would be in everyone's best interests.

As he reached the old Munford place, he braked to a stop. He peered through the white stuff filling the air and surveyed the ramshackle old house that was on the verge of falling in on itself. When he'd been a kid, Hal Munford and his wife Lanita had lived there. The couple had been ancient even then. No kids. The property had gone to a nephew of Hal's who lived in California, but he'd never come to collect any of the belongings there. He paid the taxes and that was about it.

Garrett eased off the road into what had once been a narrow drive. The old house was close to the road so he didn't have to go far. He climbed out of the truck and scanned the area. The roar of the river that ran along the other side of the road was nearly deafening in the otherwise silence. Like any barn or structure this close to the crime scene, the deserted house had been checked earlier today but it didn't hurt to have another look. Particularly considering it was this close to Abbey's place and that treehouse recently used for shelter by an unknown person.

He made his way to the house. No tracks in the snow. A good sign. The front door was already open, probably from whoever had searched it earlier. The weathered door barely hung on to the frame by a single hinge. Inside the house were four rooms, all stripped bare save for a random chair or side table. The kitchen had no built-in cabinets and whatever pieces had been lined up against the walls for storage were long gone. Either sold at auction or given away, maybe stolen over the years as the house deteriorated.

He saw no indication that anyone had been inside. Snow filtered in through the broken windows, creating little drifts here and there on the wide plank wood floor. He walked to the second of the two bedrooms, the only room he hadn't checked. The house didn't have a bathroom but at one time there had been an outhouse in the back.

Garrett stilled in the open doorway. There was more snow in this room. The one window didn't have just a few broken panes like the other windows in the house, this one was missing the entire lower sash. He crossed to the window and peered out into the snow that pretty much obscured his view now.

Fresh tracks that were quickly filling with snow marred the white blanket.

"Son of a..."

Garrett climbed out the window, his phone already at his ear as he put through a call to Wagner. He rushed through the snow, following the tracks that would all too soon disappear. Whoever had been here hadn't been gone long. Maybe a couple of minutes.

"I was just about to call you, Sheriff," Wagner said by way of a greeting.

"I'm at the old Munford place," Garrett said over the lashing of the wind and the sound of rushing water. "Someone's been here in the last few minutes." He reached the tree line of the woods that bordered the property and the tracks vanished.

"Sending help your way, Sheriff."

Garrett moved into the woods more slowly, alternately scanning the ground and surveying the area around him. "I'm thinking whoever was here heard me pull up and took off out the bedroom window. He headed into the woods. I've lost his trail."

Damn it. He turned all the way around, the snow swirling down around him as if he'd stepped into a shaken snow globe.

"Tracey and Nelson are en route to your location," Wagner said. "You should probably stand down, Sheriff, until you have back up."

Garrett remained as still as possible, moving nothing but his eyes from side to side, watching for the slightest movement. "Let them know I'm at the tree line behind the house."

That was the instant that Garrett's attention settled on the broken-down barn that sat only a few yards from the tree line about halfway between his position and the house. He turned in that direction. Whoever had fled into the woods when he arrived, could have circled back and entered the barn.

"I know that silence," Wagner warned, "what's happening, Sheriff?"

"I'm going into the barn," Garrett said in a near whisper.

"You mean there's some part of it that's still standing?" The disbelief in his deputy's voice didn't slow Garrett's stride in that direction.

He didn't bother answering. He couldn't hope for the element of surprise since the structure had enough cracks in the partially standing walls to throw a stick of firewood through. But he wasn't going out of his way to warn whoever might be inside.

He moved in at the rear of the structure, the part that was closest to the woods. A couple of missing boards in the siding allowed him to see inside. The light coming in through the missing parts of the roof allowed him to see fairly well. Snow covered most of the ground inside. No tracks as best he could see. He moved to a larger opening and ducked inside.

He progressed cautiously through the building, his gaze

roving the ground for any sign of human tracks and the dark corners for any flicker of movement.

"I need to hear your voice, Sheriff."

Garrett had forgotten he still had Wagner on the line. "Nothing in the barn. No sign anyone's been holed up here or in the house, but someone has definitely passed through." He explained about the treehouse and what Abbey found there. "Could have been a hunter," he said before his deputy could suggest as much, "but seeing those tracks leading away from the old Munford house this close to our homicide scene and to Abbey makes me doubt that scenario."

"Well, here's something else to make you doubt the hunter theory," Wagner said.

Garrett moved back out into the open, snow covered ground between the house and the woods. Frustration twisted through him as he walked toward the driveway. "What's that?"

"I was about to call you when you phoned. Scott from over at the market came by. He was all excited about some guy coming into his store. It took a moment to get him calmed down so he could tell me who."

A patrol car pulled into the driveway and two deputies emerged. Tracey and Nelson. With the roads icing quickly, the two had obviously been close by or they would still be minutes away. Garrett asked Wagner, "So who was it?"

"He can't be positive, mind you," Wagner warned. "Scott said he only got a glance at his profile as he walked out of the store, but he showed the cashier who waited on him a photo and she said it was the same guy."

Garrett felt like reaching through the phone line and shaking his deputy. "Wagner, who was it?"

"Steven Gray. Scott said if it wasn't him it was his identical twin."

A new kind of tension twisted through Garrett. "How

recent was this photo?" Garrett doubted the man had seen Gray in fifteen years. It was highly unlikely anyone in the community had.

"The picture was from an article in the Billings Gazette about when he was released from prison last year. Scott said he was as sure as he could be that it was him considering he hadn't seen his whole face, but the cashier was positive."

Could still have been someone else, but Garrett wasn't prepared to take the risk.

"I need to let Abbey know about this," he said, his pulse accelerating. "I'll leave Tracey and Nelson to look around here."

Abbey might believe she could take care of herself, but her mother had probably believed the same thing.

No one knew what he or she would do when face-to-face with a killer, especially when it was someone you should be able to trust.

CHAPTER EIGHT

3:55 p.m.

ABBEY POURED out the dregs in the bottom of her last cup of coffee. She'd had enough. More than enough. She filled her cup with water and headed back to the living room. At the front window she stared out at the wintry scene.

Perfect. Pure white. So beautiful. She'd always loved the snow against the backdrop of the woods that circled her childhood home. Most of the trees were evergreens, their limbs heavy with clouds of snow. It would be dark soon and the temperature would plummet.

How could something so beautiful be so lethal? Winter storm Holly was creating serious problems every place it touched. She was grateful for the supplies from the market Garrett had dropped off. The cold permeated the glass, making her shiver. Her arms went automatically around her waist.

Maybe she should have listened to him about going into town or to the ranch. It wasn't that she didn't have what she needed to get through the storm. Channel 31 was forecasting that Holly would move on out within the next twenty-four hours. That seemed to be the storm's speed. It lingered anywhere from twenty to thirty or so hours wherever it blustered its way into. There was talk of a warm front coming not so far behind Holly, but it was too early to be sure it would follow the same path.

Abbey could be stuck here for a while. Didn't matter. Not really. She had plenty to do. She glanced at the fireplace and decided to pile on another log. She'd brought in several armloads of firewood after Garrett left. No need to wait until the weather grew worse. She had coffee, bottled water in the event the pipes under the house froze, and food for several days. After what happened at the treehouse, she'd rounded up a box of shells for the shotgun. She hoped she wouldn't need the one in the chamber, much less more.

Rather than stand around staring out the window just waiting for trouble to arrive, she decided to start packing. The photo albums and keepsakes were first on her agenda. She'd already prepared three small and two medium size boxes. The ticking of the old grandfather clock made her feel much more at home. After hauling in the wood, she'd walked around the house trying to put her finger on what it was that seemed to be off. The quiet was, she'd realized, too quiet. Last night she'd been too tired to notice and then this morning Garrett had arrived with his shocking news. Finally, she'd realized it was the grandfather clock. It had belonged to her great grandparents. The antique grandfather clock had stood in the house for Abbey's entire life, but it hadn't been wound since her father died. She'd wound the clock and eased the hands to the correct hour and minute, going through the chimes until the time and the chimes were synced just as her father had taught her.

That missing tick-tock was what had felt off.

The crunch of snow and the idle of an engine drew her attention back to the window. She crossed the room and spotted the Park County Sheriff's Department truck rolling to a stop in front of her house.

Garrett.

What was he doing back here? She'd wondered if he would call and check on her before the night was over or maybe even bring pizza as he'd suggested. But after she'd insisted she could take care of herself and that he should focus on his investigation, she'd decided he might not. He'd also mentioned assigning a detail to keep an eye on her place which she felt was unnecessary and she'd said as much. In any event, he was here. She would see what he had to say.

Hopefully no one else had been murdered. She shuddered at the idea.

As he climbed the steps, she unlocked the door and opened it wide for him to come in. "Back so soon?" She smiled, hoping he wouldn't take the comment the wrong way.

Funny, growing up they'd practically been able to read each other's minds. Things were different now. They were all grown up and hardly saw each other more than once a year. His gaze settled on hers and the worry there warned this was not just a drop by to see how she was doing. Something else had happened.

Renewed worry pushed into her chest.

He removed his hat and held it in his hands as if he needed to ensure they were occupied. "Have you heard from Steven?"

A frown tugged at her brow. "What? No. I've already told you this. You said he didn't show up for work but that's the last I heard. Has he contacted you?"

"No, but he was spotted in town." Garrett shrugged. "Scott Pearson at the market believes he saw him. The cashier who rung up the guy IDed him as Steven from a photo taken last year when he was released from prison."

Abbey remembered the photo and the accompanying article. It was the first time she'd seen her brother's face in fifteen years. He looked so much like their father. Handsome, square jaw. Same hair and eyes. She blinked the memory away.

"Then he's here." A mixture of anticipation and uncertainty churned inside her. She didn't know whether to be afraid or cautiously optimistic.

"It seems so."

Good grief. She stared at Garrett's coat. "I'm sorry." She gestured to his broad shoulders. "Take off your coat. Would you like water or," she shrugged, "something stronger?"

She had wine but unless he'd changed, Garrett was a beer guy who indulged in the occasional whiskey. Tucked beneath the kitchen sink was a bottle of her father's favorite bourbon. He'd rarely touched the stuff but there were occasions when it was needed. This seemed like one of those times.

"Thanks but I'd like to check on Mr. Hansen, and I don't really want to leave you here alone."

There it was. His refusal to believe that she could take care of herself. "I thought you were sending someone to watch after me. Not that I need someone watching after me, mind you." She'd lived in the big city for years now. There wasn't a whole lot she was afraid of and she definitely knew how to take care of herself in most situations.

"If you won't go to the ranch with me," Garrett announced, "I'm staying here with you. I just need to check in at the Hansen place first."

Was he serious? The sheer determination in his brown eyes warned he was indeed. A half dozen valid arguments raced to the tip of her tongue, but she knew Garrett Gilmore entirely too well to believe she could win this battle. He'd made up his mind and there would be no changing it.

And maybe she didn't want him to.

Rather than dissect that thought, she said, "All right. Give me a sec to get my coat and boots."

In the kitchen, she took her coat from its hook by the back door and pulled it on. While she tugged on her gloves, she pushed one foot and then the other into her boots. She checked the deadbolt on the door and grabbed her keys from the counter. Garrett waited right where she'd left him.

"Watch the steps," he said as he opened the front door and stepped out onto the porch. "They're getting a little icy."

She locked the door and poked the keys into her pocket. "I'll put something on them when we get back."

Living in an apartment all these years, she'd grown accustomed to someone else taking care of those sorts of things. She should have already sprinkled de-icer on the front and the back steps. Then again, after bringing in the firewood she hadn't expected to go outside again much less have company. With the weather growing worse every hour, there wouldn't be many people out and about.

Except Garrett.

Law enforcement, she amended with a glance at the man who opened the passenger side door of his truck. Garrett wouldn't sleep a wink until this storm was over. He and his deputies would do all within their power to see that the residents of Park County were safe.

Before she could climb in the truck the cold had invaded her outer wear, making her shiver. She settled into the seat and fastened her safety belt. Her father had raved about what a great sheriff Garrett was. Better than anyone before him. So caring. So dedicated. So considerate. She wouldn't have expected any less from him.

Abbey stared at his profile as he slid behind the wheel. And handsome. The day's beard growth on his jaw made her want to reach out and slide her fingers over those planes and angles. She shook off the idea and faced forward. All during high school the girls had chased after him as if he were a rock star. No matter how pretty or popular the girl, he was always careful how he reacted. Always kind and yet noncommittal. As if he'd enjoyed the attention but hadn't wanted to give anyone the wrong idea or string any of his admirers along. His dark hair was shorter now, barely touching his collar. His body was broader and more muscular, but still lean. He'd hit six feet when he was seventeen. By the time he was twenty he'd grown another couple of inches. The cowboy boots and hat made him appear even taller.

But beneath the handsome exterior and the cowboy trappings, he was still the same old nice guy he'd been as a kid.

She turned back to him. "Why in the world aren't you married?"

The question popped out of her mouth rather than flitting through her mind. She could have bitten off her tongue. Heat rushed up her neck and she instantly stared straight ahead once more.

"I could ask you the same thing."

He looked at her now instead of the snow-covered road. She didn't have to turn her head to know, she felt his gaze on her.

"I'm too...busy," she sputtered. She dropped her head against the back of the seat and silently ranted at herself. There were many reasons why she remained single and being busy wasn't at the top of the list.

Could she have answered anymore generically?

The resounding silence that followed didn't help.

Finally, he said, "I get it. I should mind my own business."

She shouldn't have been, but she was immensely grateful he totally misunderstood. When was the last time she'd allowed herself to get flustered in the presence of anyone, much less someone she'd known her entire life? Thankfully he turned down the drive to the Hansen home before she had to answer.

The house sat back in the woods a full quarter of a mile from the road, much like her childhood home. In fact, if they'd cut through the woods instead of taking the road, they could have arrived more quickly. Except they would have had to go on foot and with the storm, that wasn't feasible.

A county cruiser sat in the snow-covered driveway a few yards from the house. Mr. Hansen's truck was likely around back the way she'd parked her SUV at home.

As much as Abbey would prefer to stay right here in Garrett's truck, that would be disrespectful. She owed it to Mr. Hansen to offer her condolences. He and his wife had been good neighbors and friends to her family for as long as she could remember.

"Mr. Hansen didn't want to leave home either," Abbey guessed. The man had lived in this house, on this land from the day a midwife helped him into the world. Her father had done the same. Though Hansen's wife was gone now, her things were here...her essence still lingered in the house. Abbey sensed her father's essence even a year after his death.

"We were able to sequester him in the bedroom until the forensic folks were done, but we couldn't convince him to leave the house except to follow his wife to the morgue." Garrett shut off the engine. "Can't blame him, I guess."

"He doesn't have anyone left? What about—?"

"He didn't want to go to his sister's," Garrett explained before she finished. "My deputy said she called and spoke to him. She was too afraid to get out in the storm and at her age she shouldn't."

Abbey understood. He was devastated and this storm wasn't helping. "There's never a good time to die." She stared out the windshield at the tsunami of snow. "But there are certainly worse times."

"No kidding."

Before she could climb out, he was already at her door offering his hand. They walked to the house together. His deputy opened the door to greet them.

"Sheriff," the older man said as he pulled the door open wider.

He looked familiar. Abbey glanced at his name tag and smiled. "Deputy Johnson."

He was the one who had found her father. Her father had been on a ladder repairing a piece of soffit on the house. He'd fallen, hit his head and died from exposure before he was found. The guilt she'd almost gotten under control twisted deep in her heart. She hadn't been here for him. She'd been on a book tour and hadn't taken the time to call that evening.

"Abbey." The deputy gave her a nod. "Good to see you again."

Lionel Hansen appeared in the doorway that led into the hall and the bedrooms on that side of the house. "Abbey." He suddenly stiffened as if he'd had to resist his initial impulse to reach out to her the way he would have in the past. He turned his attention to Garrett then. "Sheriff."

"I wanted to check once more before the roads become completely impassible," Garrett said. "Are you certain you don't want to go to Belgrade and stay with your sister?"

Mr. Hansen shook his head. "I'm not leaving." He glanced at Abbey again. "I know the storm is creating issues for your investigation, but all I want is for you to find out who killed my wife."

"I'm so sorry," Abbey said, her heart aching for the man. His wife had been so nice. Every holiday after her mother was gone she'd brought homemade cookies to Abbey.

"You know," he said to her, his gray eyes strangely cold, "my wife was murdered around the same time you showed up.

I've been thinking about that all day. I just can't see it as a coincidence."

"Mr. Hansen, I understand you're..."

Garrett was responding to the man's unexpected comment, but Abbey's brain couldn't seem to assimilate the words. She could only stare at the man who had known her since she was born. How could he think she would have anything to do with hurting his wife?

Steven was her brother. She supposed Mr. Hansen might believe she had some knowledge of her brother's whereabouts.

"I haven't seen my brother," she said, interrupting whatever Garrett was saying. "Not in fifteen years. We haven't spoken in all that time. Whatever you're thinking, you're wrong."

"Like my Dottie was wrong when your mother was murdered?" he countered, his voice rising with fury. "That low down brother of yours called her a liar."

Garrett stepped between them, severing the visual contact. "Mr. Hansen, you're emotional right now. You're not thinking clearly. Abbey would never be involved in hurting anyone."

"I read her books," he fairly shouted.

The force of his words had Abbey backing up a step. What was he implying?

"Seems to me she's got all kinds of evil thoughts in that head of hers."

She couldn't believe what she was hearing. How could he say such a thing? She wrote fiction. Suspense. Clearly Garrett was right, the man was emotional and not thinking clearly. There simply was no other explanation.

"Stay in the house," Garrett was saying to Hansen. "Listen to what Deputy Johnson says and we'll get through this storm and back to what needs to be done as quickly as possible."

Hansen stamped out of the room.

Garrett turned to Abbey. "I'm sorry. I should have anticipated he might react this way. They were married for most of
their lives. He's in a kind of shock."

Feeling sad and defeated, there was nothing to do but
shake her head. "I said what I needed to say. I can wait in the
truck."

Garrett held up a hand. "Give me a minute and we'll go
together. I just need to speak with Johnson a moment."

"I'll follow you out," the deputy offered.

Abbey was already at the door before Garrett had finished
pulling on his coat. The three of them exited the house.
Garrett followed her to the truck and held her door while she
climbed into the passenger seat as if she were too fragile to
do so without assistance after the encounter with Hansen.

"I'll just be a minute," he said before closing the door.

She watched as he and Johnson huddled in the snow and
carried on a conversation that seemed to be mostly one
sided. Garrett was likely filling the other man in on the
sighting of Steven. Abbey shifted her gaze, stared out her
window. She didn't want to go through this again. She
exhaled a foggy breath. The thought was entirely selfish. Mr.
Hansen assuredly hadn't wanted his wife to be murdered
either. Of course, Steven was the most logical suspect. She'd
told herself this repeatedly. If he'd dared to show up in
Livingston or elsewhere in Park County, then he was putting
himself in the middle of this whether he was guilty or not.
Her brother wasn't stupid; he had to know that would be the
case.

The men broke the huddle. Johnson went back into the
house and Garrett climbed into the driver's seat.

"Sorry for the delay," he said as he started the engine.

"You had to bring him up to speed about Steven."

"That," he agreed, "and the fact that someone was at the

old Munford place. I'm concerned it could be the same person who was in the treehouse."

Her brother, he didn't add.

The few minutes it took to drive to her house elapsed in silence. Abbey suddenly wondered why she hadn't just hired someone to pack up and ship the things she wanted to keep and then donate or auction everything else.

She shouldn't have come back.

Of course, that would have been impossible. She needed to see things and decide for herself. There were far too many treasures and mementoes she had forgotten to risk allowing someone else to go through the history of the family she'd once had.

The realization hurt with a fresh vengeance.

Garrett parked. "This is not your fault, Abbey. Whatever happened to Mrs. Hansen, you had nothing to do with it."

"Too bad you and I are probably the only people in this county who believe that's the case. It's going to be just like last time all over again."

She got out, battled the bitter wind and snow to reach the porch. She unlocked the door without looking back. No need. Garrett was close behind her. She felt his nearness despite the freezing cold wind.

"It'll be dark in the next half hour," Garrett said as he pulled off his coat and hung it up. "Are you set with firewood for the night?"

She hung her coat next to his. "I brought plenty inside earlier."

"Good." He glanced at the dwindling flames in the fireplace. "I'll get the fire going again. Don't argue with me about this. I'm staying."

This was sure to be a long night. He was right. It was almost dark. He should stay. She shivered, still chilled by just walking those few yards through the snow. It wasn't entirely the snow. Or the wind. She hugged her arms around her waist. History seemed determined to repeat itself and that chilled her to the bone.

She went to the kitchen and removed her boots and socks. While Garrett was still stoking the flames, she went to her room and pulled on a pair of dry socks. When she returned to the living room, he had pulled off his own boots and was warming his sock clad feet near the roaring fire. No matter how good the boots, in this kind of weather some amount of dampness was bound get through even if only by condensation.

"Would you like a pair of my father's socks?"

"Not necessary. These will dry quickly enough." He flashed her a smile. "I wouldn't pass on a cup of coffee though."

"Sure. Give me five minutes."

By the time the smell of coffee filled the air, Abbey couldn't resist having a cup herself no matter that she'd had too many already. Sleep likely wasn't coming for her without significant prodding with a bottle of wine.

Garrett appeared next to her and leaned a hip against the counter. "What is it you do in the big city when you're not *too busy*?"

She laughed, couldn't help herself. Somehow she'd known he wouldn't let the comment go. "I spend a lot of time doing research for my work."

She placed two mugs on the counter and filled one, then the other. She passed one to him and cradled the other. "I go to dinner with friends and colleagues. Reporters, sometimes. Bloggers. Do the occasional reading or speaking engagement." She shrugged. "And I work. A lot."

Like she should be doing right now.

He downed a slug of coffee. "No boyfriend? Fiancé?"

She sipped her coffee then shook her head. "I date occasionally, but nothing serious. I've been too focused on my career, I suppose."

He stared at her for a long moment and she had to steel herself to prevent the awareness coursing through her to manifest itself in a shiver. It was too late at this point to blame the cold.

"You're beautiful, successful. Hell, you're a celebrity. How can you not be inundated with guys wanting to spend time with you?"

Now she really laughed. "There are lots of women far more *beautiful*," she said this with a roll of her eyes, "and successful in New York." She shook her head. "Trust me, I am not inundated with suitors."

"Hard to believe." He placed his mug on the counter and stared at her as if he'd asked a question and was anticipating her answer.

Rather than give him the chance, she asked her own. "What about you? You're still single. I suppose you're too busy as well."

He snagged his coffee and swallowed a gulp. "I never date the same woman more than a couple of times."

Abbey raised her eyebrows. "I'm sure you don't mean that the way it sounds."

He blinked then shook his head. "No, I mean I don't want anyone getting the wrong idea. Women—some women—get the wrong idea after a couple of dates."

"I see." She nodded. "So, *you* are inundated with suitors."

He laughed, but then his face and those dark eyes turned serious. "Not really, but even if I was it wouldn't matter. I guess I never got over the one who got away."

Abbey's heart kicked into a faster rhythm and she had to turn away. Was he talking about her? Probably not. She went to the sink and poured out the rest of her coffee. Surely not.

She would know, wouldn't she? "I've had far too much of this already. I'll never sleep tonight."

Did she want him to be referring to her?

When she would have moved away from the sink, he stepped in beside her with his own cup. "Maybe you can tell me about your new book."

He stood so close and the tension between them sparked with new potency.

His cell phone chirped. For a moment she feared he wasn't going to answer it and would instead continue staring at her with an intensity that made it hard to breathe.

He reached for his phone, checked the screen, then walked away.

Abbey managed a breath. She closed her eyes and regathered her wits. They had been friends for so long...they'd shared everything until she moved away. Even on her visits to her father, Garrett had always made time to take her to dinner or to just sit around talking, catching up.

But this didn't feel like friendship. This felt like far more. As if they'd moved through some thin barrier that separated the warmth and familiarity they'd always shared from something hot and fierce...visceral.

Her father's warning that she couldn't ignore her personal needs forever echoed in her mind. He'd always hoped she and Garrett would end up together. As a college student she'd been incensed by his persistent optimism on the subject. She had big plans and those plans didn't include coming back to Park County to spend the rest of her life. She'd needed to be away from this place. Away from the memories...from the way people had looked at her even long after that awful day.

Garrett came back into the kitchen, his face clean of whatever might be on his mind. "I'm ready to hear about your new work in progress." He rinsed his mug, filled it with water and drank it down.

Despite her best efforts she watched his hand, his throat and then his lips as he lowered the mug to the sink next to hers.

She blinked away the images. "Everything okay?" If there had been another sighting of Steven she would like to know.

"My deputies didn't find anything at the Munford property. For the next few hours we'll be focusing primarily on keeping folks safe as this storm sweeps through. I'll probably get calls all night. I'm hoping there won't be any accidents or anyone going missing."

She imagined he would be up most of the night. Which meant she needed to be in her own room *sleeping*. She would tell him about her story over dinner and then she was putting a few walls between them. This unfamiliar territory had unnerved her.

Though she might never be back in Park County, Garrett was a dear friend. She didn't want to risk ruining that with something impulsive.

"Since you promised to bring pizza when you came back," she reminded him, "you're lucky I had a frozen one delivered today."

"You pretty much let me know you'd be fine without me around. I figured the pizza was off..." He shrugged, then smiled. "But, hey, I'm happy to preheat the oven."

She laughed, felt a little of the unfamiliar tension slip away. "Deal."

While he prepared the oven, she dug out the pizza pan and removed the frozen entrée from its packaging. She told him about her latest project and her hopes for what came next in her career. He appeared enthralled by her every word. This made her inordinately happy.

When the pizza was done, she opened a bottle of wine and they moved into the living room. He took the sofa and she settled in her mother's chair.

"Since I missed the ten-year reunion, why don't you catch me up on all the gossip?"

"My mother," he said on a laugh, "recounts what every classmate we had is doing about once a month." At Abbey's confused expression, he explained, "It's her way of reminding me that I'm not married and have not provided her with any grandchildren."

Abbey laughed as much from his resigned expression as from his mother's persistence. He brought her up to speed on who was married and who had children. Who was divorced and who had moved away. Sadly, he was correct. It was a little depressing in one sense. Mostly it was funny and real and familiar. Then the trip down memory lane really began. Oh, the stories they could both tell but she was more than satisfied allowing him to do the telling.

She couldn't remember when she'd laughed so much as she devoured slices of pizza and drank wine. With all that was going on in his county Garrett stuck with water. Didn't matter. She consumed enough wine for the both of them, just listening to him talk. Watching his lips as he spoke. Relishing the way his eyes lit up whenever he talked about some of the most memorable times they had shared.

Before she knew it, she was the one talking and he was doing the watching and listening.

That was the moment...the moment she saw in his eyes what she understood deep inside.

There would never be a serious relationship or a special someone.

Because he was here and she was there and this bond between them refused to be severed by time or distance.

Instead, it grew stronger and stretched into new territory.

LIVINGSTON 31 NEWS

Camille Dutton had never been so cold in her life. She stood just inside the doors of Gil's bar at the historic Murray Hotel. Christmas lights twinkled in every window. Since darkness had crept in, Livingston had become a ghost town. Snowdrifts banked against anything not moving. Trees, buildings, vehicles. It was a mess. She could just imagine how bad it would be by morning. Snowplows were doing all possible to clear the roads, but the sheer volume of snow was overwhelming. Guests from the hotel were hanging out in the bar, but Camille didn't mind an audience. She'd had a change of clothes and freshened her makeup since her last broadcast. She was good to go.

Since Garrett hadn't returned her calls, she'd spoken to his deputy sheriff, Kyle Wagner. According to Kyle, Garrett was staying close to this morning's homicide scene. Camille was relatively certain that wasn't entirely accurate since Scott Pearson had told her about Garrett offering to drop off a delivery to Abbey Gray. Camille had already heard that Abbey was back in town. Those who knew the two had told Camille that everyone had always suspected there was something more than friendship between them. More likely, Garrett was staying close to his old flame. Oh well, Garrett had made it abundantly clear he wasn't interested in a relationship. Whatever, she had bigger plans than this two-horse town anyway.

The thing that really got under her skin was the idea that she could be reporting on a murder instead of this storm if Garrett had bothered to give her a heads up. At least the storm was national news. She'd be getting some major face time across the country for this. Reporting on some old woman who was murdered in her backyard wouldn't have done much for her career. Still, he could have at least told her about it.

"And we're live in," her cameraman announced, "three, two one."

"Holly has certainly lived up to her promise, friends. In some areas as much as three feet of snow has fallen already. Roads are impassable. Snowplows are out in full force, but they can't stay ahead of the snow that continues to fall. I've checked in with the Park County Sheriff's Department and we've been very lucky so far. No known casualties related to the storm. The north western part of the state hasn't been so lucky. Stay off the roads, please. Stay in your homes. By noon tomorrow Holly will be forging a path through Wyoming. The Jackson Hole Airport has already closed due to the wind and snow. For now, folks, everything in Livingston and the surrounding area is closed to ride out the storm."

Camille pressed a hand to her chest. "I urge you to please stay inside. We're hovering at fourteen degrees, but it feels far colder with the wind still gusting a good thirty miles an hour. Unfortunately, it's going to get worse before it gets better."

She smiled, showing off the gleaming white teeth she worked so hard to keep that way and infused pride into her expression. "A special thanks to Sheriff Garrett Gilmore for ensuring that folks living in the farthest corners of the county are safe. You're our hero tonight, Sheriff. This is Camille Dutton with Channel 31 News. Back to the studio."

CHAPTER NINE

GARRETT SAT UP.

The fading flames of the fire flickered in the dark room.

He threw aside the blanket and listened. The faint crackle amid the ashes and embers was scarcely audible with the sound of the wind roaring outside. A distinct moan echoed from the old house.

He checked his phone. No calls, no messages. It was nearly midnight. Hopefully this was a good sign. If they could get through the next few hours without anyone getting trapped out in this storm, he'd consider himself damned lucky. The worst would be over by noon tomorrow. Another dozen hours and he could breathe easy.

The house whispered an uneasy groan in the silence. The weight of snow on the roof, the force of the wind played havoc with houses and barns and various other structures. This was something else he hoped they'd escape: serious property damage. There were those who couldn't afford insurance and a storm like this could ruin them.

Garrett stood. He was surprised he'd managed two whole hours of sleep. Abbey had decided to call it a night early. She'd gone upstairs by nine, citing she was still on eastern time.

As much as he hated to admit it, he was thankful. He'd been on the verge of confessing the renewed feelings churning inside since he'd heard she was back in Park County. He was a damned fool, but he'd sensed she felt something too. He shook his head, ran his hands through his hair. The idea was maybe a little on the irrational side. Abbey Gray had no time for him. She was *busy*. Like she said.

She lived on the other side of the country. Might as well be on the other side of the world. He exhaled a big breath. He searched for news about her on the internet far more often than he would like to admit. She was always surrounded by adoring fans, many of whom were male. She had an exciting, international life. Hell, she'd spent the summer on a book tour in Europe. What in the world did he have to offer her?

But there was that moment when Channel 31 cut in with a weather bulletin and Camille Dutton had given him that shout out. Abbey had looked surprised or taken aback. He'd immediately explained that he and Camille had dated. She was the reason he'd learned to be more careful about dating. He hadn't meant to lead Camille on. Even after three months since they'd last had dinner, she still took every opportunity to flirt with him.

He should be flattered but mostly he was concerned. The folks in this county expected him to be a man of integrity in his personal life as well as on the job. He sure didn't want Abbey thinking there was something more between him and Camille. Particularly not if some chance of the two of them moving their relationship to a new level even remotely existed.

Shaking off the foolish notion, he righted his shirt, pulled his weapon from beneath the pillow Abbey had provided and tucked it into his waistband. Maybe he would make a fresh pot of coffee. Check in with dispatch.

He stretched his back and padded to the front window in his sock feet. The snow was still coming down. Fast and hard. He yawned and shuffled into the kitchen. He checked the door out of habit and peered beyond the glass panes. The blanket of white had thickened on the ground, done a hell of a good job of camouflaging her SUV.

He flipped on the overhead light and went through the steps of preparing the coffee. He pressed brew and walked to the other end of the kitchen to look out the two windows beyond the table and chairs. Nothing to see but more snow and trees cloaked in the white stuff. A winter wonderland.

A dangerous one.

Pacing back to the living room, he paused at the bottom of the stairs. He hadn't heard a peep from the second floor. With any luck she was still asleep, and her door was closed. The smell of the coffee brewing might wake her otherwise.

Maybe he should check.

His memory served him well as he skipped steps number four and number ten. Those were the ones that creaked. As soundlessly as possible, he padded along the upstairs hall. Steven's room was on the right. Abbey's was a couple yards down on the left. Before he could analyze his actions, Garrett paused at her brother's bedroom door, opened it. He flipped on the light, blinked to adjust his eyes. Everything looked the same as it had when eighteen-year-old Steven Gray lived here. Celebrity athletic posters on the wall. Headphones still lying on the bed. Trophies on a shelf above his bed reminded

Garrett that Abbey's brother had been a star baseball player all through high school.

Garrett frowned, surveyed the trophies again. Where was the bat he'd used in the playoffs that year? The coach had it engraved with the year and the score and mounted on a plaque. The plaque was still there but no bat.

He'd have to ask Abbey if she'd noticed anything missing.

He turned off the light and moved on to her room. He knew the space beyond that door as well as his own room at home.

Since her door was closed, he turned to go. Before he could she stepped out of the room.

He stalled.

She made a sound, not quite a squeal but something on that order.

"I wanted...sorry. I didn't mean to wake you." His shoulders slumped. He'd certainly bumbled that attempt.

"You didn't wake me. I think the wind did. I was just lying there thinking about Steven and then I smelled the coffee."

As she spoke his gaze drifted down to her lips, then dropped farther to the nightshirt she wore. She'd never been the pajama or nightgown type. Just a big old comfy tee. Nothing fancy.

Her arms wrapped around her breasts. He blinked, jerked his attention upward.

"Is everything okay?" she asked pointedly as if she'd already asked the question and he'd failed to answer.

Because he'd been staring at the form of her breasts beneath the thin fabric.

"Yeah." He nodded. "Everything's good."

Everything except his ability to keep his head on straight.

"I'll join you for coffee then."

She gave him her back and returned to her bed. A moment of confusion kept him from moving. When she pulled on a robe he recognized as her father's she walked back to the door.

They were going downstairs. For coffee.

Evidently, he needed the caffeine more than he'd realized.

He cleared his throat. "You probably wake up in the middle of the night from time to time with an idea for one of your stories."

She laughed. "More often than you know."

He followed her down the stairs. His fingers itched to reach out and touch her tousled hair. The long tresses were still the same silky blond as when she was a kid. Along with the light hair she had the bluest eyes. Both were vivid in the photo on the inside cover flaps of her books. The unedited, totally Abbey shot had been taken on the steps of an old brownstone. She'd looked seventeen in those faded jeans and the pale blue sweater. And her feet were bare, resting against the vintage brick. That may have been his favorite part.

In the kitchen she poured the coffee. Since she'd said she had been thinking about Steven, he asked, "Are you concerned he'll show up at your door?"

She cradled her mug in both hands and considered his question. "No. I'm okay with him showing up. I guess I'm worried that maybe I was wrong about him."

The possibility had crossed Garrett's mind more than once since this morning. "We might never know for sure."

Her gaze met his and the worry there made him ache to reassure her.

"But if I was wrong all those years ago, that could mean he was the one who..."

Garrett held up a hand before she voiced the rest of her fear. "We don't need to go there right now." He thought of the missing baseball bat. "Have you noticed anything missing in the house?"

She shook her head, then stopped mid shake. "Mother's

pearls. I'm sure they're around here somewhere but I haven't found them yet." Her eyes closed for a second before she went on. "I keep thinking about the way Mr. Hansen looked at me. The cold..." She winced. "Hatred. It was so obvious. He's known me my whole life, why would he feel such loathing for me?"

"He just lost his wife. He's not thinking clearly."

"You're right." She sipped her coffee. "Maybe I'm feeling guilty because deep down I understand Steven may have been involved."

Garrett wished he could find the right words to comfort her but there were none that would erase the painful possibility that her brother might be a murderer. He hoped what he was about to ask wouldn't make matters worse. "Did you or your father remove or change anything in—?"

His cell vibrated before he could finish the question. "Hold on." He snagged the cell from his back pocket. Wagner's name and face flashed on the screen. A new tension twisted through Garrett. "What's up?" he said rather than his usual greeting.

"Nothing, I hope," his deputy said but his voice told the real story. He knew something was up and whatever it was, it was not good. "Johnson didn't make his last check in. I've called him three times on his radio and twice on his cell. He's not answering. I thought about sending someone out to follow up but with the road conditions it's going to take some serious time to get there."

"You're right." Dread congealed in Garrett's gut. "I'm right next door. I can get over there a whole lot faster."

"When you reach the Hansen house, I want a call from you ASAP," Wagner urged. "Snowplows are working overtime so the sand and aggregate trucks can do their job, but it's bad out there, Garrett. Really bad. We've been lucky so far that folks are staying in, but that could change anytime. If something has happened at the Hansen place, I need you to stay safe."

He wasn't telling Garrett anything he didn't know but he got the message: they could not afford to lose anyone to this weather or to this case. Everyone was needed to get through this.

"I'm on my way."

He ended the call and slid his phone back into his hip pocket. "I have to go next door and check on things. Johnson isn't picking up his phone or his radio. I need to make sure he and Mr. Hansen are doing okay."

The catch in her breath warned him that Abbey feared the worst the same way he did.

She plopped her mug on the counter. "Give me two minutes, I'll go with you."

"I don't want you out there." When she would have argued, he said, "I don't have time to debate this. I need you to do exactly what I say."

"All right." She pulled the lapels of the robe closer to her throat. "Tell me what you need me to do."

"I want you to get dressed. Boots, the works. Just in case you have to leave in a hurry. Then I want you to sit at the bottom of that staircase with your daddy's shotgun and that box of ammo." He nodded to the kitchen table where the box she'd rounded up still sat. "If anyone tries to come through a door or a window, I want you to shoot. Don't ask questions. Don't hesitate. Just shoot."

She nodded, then sprinted out of the kitchen. The sound of her rushing up the stairs set him in motion.

He pulled on his boots, then his utility belt and holstered his weapon. By the time his coat was on and zipped to the throat, she was at the bottom of the stairs once more. She hurried into the kitchen and returned with her boots on and her coat in her hand, then settled on the second step, the coat on one side of her and the shotgun on the other.

"Where's your phone?"

She tugged it from her hip pocket. "Fully charged."

"Good." He reached for his hat and resisted the impulse to go to her. He'd only do something he might regret like pull her into his arms and kiss her. He couldn't allow this thing to get out of hand until he was certain it wasn't stress induced. "Lock the door behind me."

He turned for the door, twisted the deadbolt and rested his hand on the knob in preparation to go.

"Garrett."

He looked back at her. She hadn't moved but the struggle to stay where she was showed in the way she leaned toward him and looked ready to lunge to her feet.

"Be careful. When this is over, we have things to talk about."

He nodded, a tightness in his throat. "You do the same."

He walked out the door without looking back. If he'd looked back, he would never have been able to leave her and he had to. He wasn't dragging her into an unknown situation.

The door closed behind him, he hesitated on the steps until he heard the lock turn. Lifting his booted feet as if he were climbing a mountain, he plowed through the snow, the wind pushing at him like a defensive lineman attempting to block a play. After swiping away enough snow to see out the windshield, he opened his truck door and climbed in. She stood at the window watching as he backed up and turned around. He headed down the drive. The snow was axle deep at this point, but four-wheel drive kept the truck moving forward.

Frozen snow and puddles of ice crunched beneath his tires as he turned onto Mill Creek. He straddled what he believed to be the middle of the road since it was nearly impossible to see where the road ended before becoming part of the river. He almost missed the turn onto the Hansen driveway.

No tracks, vehicle or otherwise, marred the knee-deep snow. If there was trouble, it hadn't walked or driven in this way. He thought of the woods that stretched along Mill Creek, connected the properties with the perfect cover for slipping from one place to the next.

As he neared the clearing where the house and barn stood, Johnson's patrol car came into view. The driver's side door was open, motor running, lights on. His gut clenched. He slammed the gearshift into Park, shut off the engine and powered down the window to listen. Wind. Patrol car motor running. Nothing else.

Garrett shoved his flashlight into his utility belt, eased out of the truck, left the door ajar rather than risk the noise of closing it. He drew his weapon and began the march through the snow. He listened intently, scanned the area left to right, right to left, over and over as he moved forward.

He spotted the blood in the snow before he saw the body.

"Son of a..."

He moved closer, couched next to the form that was his deputy. Fury tore through Garrett. Johnson's unseeing eyes stared up at the falling snow. He lay between the door and the car. Blood had filled and started to freeze in the split that parted his throat. More had soaked into his shirt and the snow beneath him, creating an icy river of crimson red.

Garrett rose to his feet, turned all the way around, watching for movement, listening for sound. He no longer felt the cold. No longer cared that the wind tugged at his hat and stung his eyes, making them water. All he felt was sheer determination and black rage.

No one appeared in his line of sight. Snow swirled from

heavily laden branches that shifted with the sway of mother nature's force.

He started forward again, moving toward the porch. Taking care, he climbed the steps and headed for the door. It was ajar.

His hopes sank.

Damn it. He did not want to find another body in here. With Johnson dead, the likelihood that Hansen was still alive was little to none.

He pushed the door inward. The lights were on. A dwindling fire flickered beyond the hearth. The only sound was the occasional crackle and pop of the embers inside and the buffeting wind outside.

Garrett entered the house, closed the door, his weapon leveled as he scanned the living room.

Clear.

He put through a call to Wagner. "Johnson is dead."

If Hansen was also dead as he suspected, it was far too easy to predict the next victim. Garrett gritted his teeth. He shouldn't have left Abbey alone.

"Backup is en route," Wagner confirmed. "Calling the coroner now."

"I want the first to arrive at the Gray house with Abbey. She's there alone."

After a quick conversation via his radio, Wagner said, "Done."

Moving to the kitchen, Garrett listened through the string of questions from his deputy—the ones he hadn't asked before dispatching backup. When Wagner had fallen silent, Garrett said, "No sign of Hansen. Put out an APB on Steven Gray. If it wasn't him Scott saw, no big deal. But if he's here, I want to find him." The BOLO on his car had garnered no results.

"Will do." Pause. "Garrett, watch your back."

"Doing my best."

Garrett put his phone away and checked the back door. Locked. He checked the windows. No broken windows on the first floor. Whoever had come in, had done so through the front door.

Who let the trouble in? Johnson would never open the door without checking first. What the hell was he doing outside? And where the hell was Hansen...or his body?

Garrett checked the coat closet and bathroom, then down the hall to the bedrooms. He moved from room to room, clear.

"Damn it."

The reality that the killer had stayed around after murdering Dottie Hansen confirmed that he knew the Hansen family. Had one or more reasons to want them dead.

The only person Garrett knew with that kind of motive was Steven Gray.

Damn it.

He moved cautiously back along the hall, his heart thundering. Living room remained clear. As he reached the last step, he pulled out his phone to call Abbey. He needed to warn her that trouble might be headed her way.

Might hell? He knew it was. He didn't want her opening the door for anyone, least of all her brother.

The blow that slammed into the back of his head sent him hurtling forward. His cell flew from his hand and slid across the floor. His fingers instinctively tightened on the butt of his weapon.

Pain shattered in his skull as he attempted to scramble to his feet.

Before he steadied himself, another blow landed and pin pricks of light flashed in his field of vision. He slumped face down on the hardwood. Boots came into view but he couldn't move...couldn't raise his head or turn his eyes to look upward.

A baseball bat thumped to the floor next to his head. Garrett tried to speak but the darkness overtook him before his lips could form the words.

CHAPTER TEN

MONDAY, December 16
12:30 a.m.

ABBEY CHECKED THE TIME AGAIN. Her nerves were jumping. Surely Garrett had made it to the Hansen place by now. He'd been gone better than fifteen minutes.

If everything was okay, why hadn't she heard from him?

The delay could only mean trouble.

She looked around the room. It was too quiet. The only sound was the clock, the familiar tick-tock she usually found comforting. Not now. Now it was a deafening reminder of each passing minute. She couldn't sit here any longer. She had to do something. Stand. Walk. Something.

Pushing to her feet and shotgun clutched in her hands, she took a breath and went to the window. The snow continued coming down so thick she could hardly see. With the moon and stars hidden by the thick cloud cover all that white stuff was the only reason it wasn't pitch black out there. She checked the door though she vividly recalled turning the deadbolt when Garrett left. *Locked.*

Her worry and frustration rising, she walked into the kitchen. Checked the deadbolt on the back door, then peered out the glass portion of the door. The white SUV she'd rented for this cross-country trip was hardly visible now.

Staring out at the fat white flakes whirling in the darkness, she thought about the intense tension that had simmered between them tonight. Admittedly, there had been moments when they were younger and even occasionally when she visited where she felt an unexpected spark or flash of warmth...a tug of something more than friends. But nothing on this level. This attraction was undeniable. Impossible to label as anything else. The pull was deep, strong.

Was it because they'd both turned thirty this year? Most of the others from their childhood had families or at least had been married. It was possible that this was nothing more than some biological nudge that time was flying past. She'd never really believed in that sort of thing. Sure she liked kids but she hadn't considered the idea of having one of her own. *Yet.*

The book was due in a few weeks.

How could she think of anything else?

How could she be here dealing with another murder and the possibility that her brother was involved? Nightmares like this weren't supposed to happen twice in a lifetime.

She closed her eyes and prayed to the God who'd never seemed to listen to her before for all the good it would do. *Please don't let this be Steven.*

The cold coming through the glass in the door reminded her to snap out of it. Staying vigilant was essential. No drifting off in thought. No worrying about something she couldn't control or change. If the worst turned out to be true, she would have to deal with it. The shotgun suddenly felt exceedingly heavy in her hands. She tightened her grip. She wasn't putting it down. In fact, she went back to the staircase and picked a few shells from the box and tucked them into her front pocket. She was a reasonably good shot—her father had seen to that—but she'd never fired at a moving target, and certainly not a human one.

Could she do it if her survival depended upon it?

Maybe.

She glanced around the room. What now?

She shivered, suddenly chilled.

Rather than continue waiting for Garrett to call her, she tucked the shotgun under her left arm and called him. He kept his phone on silent so she wasn't going to interrupt anything or give away his position if...

Not going there.

Four rings and the call went to voicemail.

She swore, hit end call. What was the number for non-emergency calls to the sheriff's department? Four oh six...

No point wasting time. She couldn't remember. She pulled up the internet and entered the info to find the number. Her heart thumped harder and harder. Something was wrong. He should have called by now.

She thought about her SUV. It would take a few minutes, but she could broom the snow off, warm it up and drive over there. But that would take too much time. And the possibility of ending up in the ditch or getting stuck in the snow was far too likely.

Better to make this call and see if dispatch had heard from him. She could be worrying for no reason. This was the sort of thing she did to characters all the time. She should be accustomed to the tension. Reviewers said she was the best at creating it.

But this was real.

"Park County Sheriff's Department."

Relief trickled through her at hearing the official voice. "This is Abbey Gray. I'm—"

"Hold on, ma'am."

The line went on hold and Abbey snapped her mouth shut. Well hell.

She paced the floor. No doubt emergency calls were coming in and she would, of course, have to wait behind those. This wasn't an emergency...she hoped.

Worry gnawed at her. Her pulse accelerated with each passing second. What was taking so long? She looked at the screen to ensure the call was still connected. Any sense of calm she'd felt at reaching dispatch vanished.

Hanging up and calling again wouldn't help unless she went the 9-1-1 route this time. Tying up that line was not appropriate...yet.

"Calm down, Abbey." She closed her eyes and told her heart to slow its pounding.

If her father was here, he would tell her there was nothing to worry about until the trouble was in front of her. In other words, don't borrow trouble. It would come along in its own time.

Miss you, Daddy.

She wished she had a number for Steven. Maybe if she called he would answer. If she could hear his voice, she would know. No matter that four years had separated them in age, she and Steven had always been close.

Would a killer have protected her and saved her the way he had all those times when she was a kid?

She closed her eyes and shook her head. The memory of speaking on that very subject nudged her. She'd told the audience at more than one of her readings that the villain could never be all bad. He or she must possess at least one redeeming quality if the character was going to touch the reader in a similar manner as the protagonist.

But her brother wasn't a character from one of her stories.

A tap on the door jerked her attention there. She rushed to the window. The Park County Sheriff's Department jacket had relief soaring through her. But it was Garrett's hat that had her setting the shotgun aside and reaching for the door.

"Ms. Gray, I need you too—" the dispatcher's voice echoed in her ear.

"Never mind," she blurted. Abbey ended the call and tucked the phone into her pocket as she twisted the deadbolt and then yanked open the door. "Thank God! I was getting worried."

Garrett raised his head, the brim of his hat coming up to reveal his face.

Not Garrett.

Steven.

Abbey reached for the shotgun. Her brother grabbed it first.

She drew back two steps. "What did you do, Steven? Where's Garrett?"

The fact that he had on Garrett's hat and coat tore at her heart. As Steven stepped inside she saw the Park County Sheriff's Department truck idling outside. Garrett's truck.

Dear God...if he'd killed Garrett.

Fury blasted away the softer emotions. "What did you do, Steven?"

He slammed the door behind him, held the shotgun in his hands but didn't take aim at her. "I came to save you."

Defeat sank inside her. "Where's Garrett?"

"He's hurt."

Fear rammed into her chest. "What did you do to him?"

"I didn't do anything to him. I used his phone to call 9-1-1. I left the line open so they would trace the call, then I grabbed his hat and came looking for you. I knew you would never open the door and listen to me if you recognized me and I need you to listen to what I have to say. We have to go, Abbey. You're not safe."

"You're wearing his hat *and* his jacket. And driving his SUV? What the hell did you do?" Her voice rose to a shout. Her body trembled with receding adrenaline. She could hardly breathe. She needed to do something. Garrett could be dying. Part of her wanted to tear into Steven but there wasn't time. "Where is he?"

Steven shook his head. His eyes wide with fear or insanity or maybe both. "I needed to be sure you'd open the door. This jacket was on the sofa in Mr. Hansen's house. I took it. I think it belonged to the dead deputy."

Dead deputy? Was he referring to Mr. Johnson? "Oh my God." Cold washed over her. "What did you do? Where's Mr. Hansen?"

"There's no time to explain," he urged. "You have to come with me."

"What are you talking about? Why would I come with you? I need to get to Garrett." She squared her shoulders and glared into the eyes that were so much darker than hers. Their father's eyes. Steven had the dark hair and dark eyes. He had the square jaw, the straight nose, the tall, wiry frame of their father. She, as her father told her so often, was the splitting image of her mother. "Shoot me or get out of my way."

"Garrett isn't dead. Believe me. But we have to get out of here. Now."

"Why?" She folded her arms over her chest. "Why would I listen to anything you have to say? I believed in you once, Steven. I won't make that mistake again."

He looked confused. Uncertain what to do next.

His bewilderment could help her escape.

"Did you take mother's pearls? I can't find them. The pearls were the one thing of hers I wanted to keep."

He blinked. Looked more confused. "What are you talking about?"

"Have you been in the house?" Of course he had. What was she thinking?

He shook his head. "I didn't get here until a few hours before dark. I came as soon as I heard what happened. I haven't been in this house since..." His expression shifted from anxious to *nothing*. A blank stare.

"I saw the stuff you left in the treehouse," she accused.

"What're you talking about?"

How could he possibly expect her to believe him? He had to be lying. There was no other explanation. "Just stop," she demanded. "Get out of my way. I'm taking the truck and going to find Garrett."

Steven's lips formed a grim line. "You have to come with me. I need to protect you. It's the only way we'll make it through this."

She held up her hands. "I don't trust anything you say. I'm not going anywhere with you." She reached for her cell phone. "I'm calling for help."

He turned the business end of the shotgun toward her. Her hand fell to her side. His face was no longer blank. Anger and determination stared back at her.

"I don't have time to try and convince you. We have to go. Now put on your coat and do what I tell you."

She got it now. Either she was going to be his ticket out of here or he had plans to kill her. If the latter was his intent, why didn't he just do it?

"I don't know what you think you're doing, but if Garrett dies," she warned, "I will kill you."

The hard words shook her. Not once in her life had she ever wanted to physically harm anyone. Not even when the whole world thought Steven had killed their mother. She'd only wanted to help him. She'd tried long and hard, but he'd pushed her away until she'd finally given up.

Now she understood that she had made a mistake.

She should never have believed in him.

The flash of surprise in his eyes shifted back into anger. "Just shut up. Shut up and listen. I couldn't save him, but I'm damned sure going to save you whether you want me to or not."

Nothing he said made sense. Was he talking about Garrett? A fresh wave of fear poured through her. "Who couldn't you save?"

"Dad. I hadn't been released yet." He drew in a harsh breath. "When I heard, I knew what had really happened."

Abbey was convinced now. Her brother really had slipped over some edge. Maybe he had years ago and she just hadn't wanted to see it. "Dad fell off a ladder doing repairs to the house, Steven."

He moved his head side to side. "No, he didn't. That's just what *he* wanted you to think. What he wanted everyone to think."

"I don't understand what you're talking about. You're not making sense." Would he shoot her if she made a run for the back door? Without her coat, how long would she last out there? "How could you possibly know anything about his death?"

"Because Dad wrote to me the day before he died. I didn't get the letter until days later and then it was too late."

Their father hadn't mentioned this to her. "He was still writing to you?"

"He hadn't written to me in years. When I got a letter after hearing that he was dead, I was a little freaked out so I read it instead of sending it back. He wanted me to know that he still believed in me but that whatever I had done he forgave me. He said he'd never stopped loving me. The day he wrote the letter he'd learned something new about Mom's death. He was really torn up about it and he was going to look into it. He said I shouldn't get my hopes up. I should just wait until I heard from him again. By the time I received his letter it didn't matter anymore."

Impossible. Her father would have called her. "If this is true," she said, still not prepared to trust him on any level, "why didn't he tell me? Why didn't you get in touch with me when you read his letter?"

"I figured I'd save us both the trouble. No one was going to listen to me. They'd just say I was making something out of nothing. So I waited. I had less than a year until I would be released. I'd waited fifteen years, what was one more?"

She couldn't continue standing here listening to whatever this was. Garrett was injured. He needed help. "I don't want to hear anymore. I'm leaving, Steven. But not with you."

His face turned as hard as stone. Then he pulled the hammer back. "One way or the other, you're going with me."

CHAPTER ELEVEN

PAIN BURST IN HIS SKULL.

Garrett's eyes opened slowly. He blinked, struggled to bring things into focus. Jumbled memories poured through his head, making it ache all the more.

He stared at the open door. The snow blowing into the room.

Blood in the snow. He jerked. Johnson was dead.

Abbey.

Garrett pressed his hands to the floor and tried to push himself upward. The room spun. He closed his eyes against the fresh wave of pain.

Get up! Get up!

Deep breath. He tried again. Made it to his knees this time. He touched the back of his head gingerly. Groaned. But he'd live.

He managed the move up to his feet. Swayed like a drunken brawler on a Saturday night binge. When he could take a step without the world moving in the opposite direction, he turned around, surveying the room.

The Hansen living room.

Tension knotted in his gut. Johnson was dead. Where was Hansen?

Garrett reached for his waist. His sidearm was still in his holster. Thank God.

Abbey. He needed to get back to her...first he had to check on Hansen.

No. First he should call it in.

He reached for his phone. Missing. The slow-motion memory of the phone flying from his hand and sliding across the floor had him scanning the room.

There.

He spotted it in the corner near the fireplace. Walking slowly, he made his way to where it lay. He braced one hand against the wall to bend down and pick up the damned thing.

It vibrated in his hand. Wagner's face flashed on his screen.

"Garrett," he said, then cleared his throat. He blinked a couple times as his vision blurred with another round and round of the room. He needed to get a hold on his equilibrium.

"Man, I'm glad to hear your voice! I thought you were dead."

Garrett licked his lips. "You weren't off by far." His gut roiled with the need to puke.

"Backup just turned onto Mill Creek. There was a semi jack-knifed on 89, held them up a bit."

Garrett started toward the front door his legs rubbery beneath him. "I'm heading to Abbey's. If Hansen is here, he's outside somewhere. Probably dead. Give the units en route a heads up to keep an eye out for Steven Gray."

"Will do. You sure you're okay?"

"Yeah." Garrett ended the call without saying more. He shoved his phone into his hip pocket and reached for the door. Where the hell was his hat? He looked back to where he'd been lying face down on the floor, didn't see it. No time.

He hurried across the porch and down the steps as quickly as he dared. The snowfall was lighter now. Thank God. At this point, he needed any break he could get. The storm moving on would be a hell of a big one.

Garrett stalled. His truck was gone. His gaze lowered to his fallen deputy who was nearly completely covered in snow now. Nausea hit him and he doubled over and vomited up the coffee he'd drank earlier. He recognized the symptoms. Concussion. Maybe worse. Couldn't worry about that right now. He made his way to where Johnson lay. As much as he wanted to move his body, he couldn't risk contaminating the crime scene. But he had to get to Abbey.

If Steven had come back and done this, he would go after her next.

"To hell with it."

Garrett leaned over Johnson and into the car. He pulled the keys from the ignition and went to the trunk to open it. The interior light blinked on. He took a moment to steel himself, then he walked back to where Johnson lay, crouched down and dug through the snow until he found the fallen man's back. He attempted to ram his arms under the body. Didn't happen. He tried again. Another wave of nausea hit him, but he forced it back. Several efforts were required to get his arms fully underneath the body and to pull him free of the ice that had formed beneath him as the snow had melted around his body when he first hit the ground.

Garrett pushed to his feet, the weight of the man's body making him sway. One staggering step at a time he made his way to the back of the car and placed Johnson in the trunk. Garrett hesitated before closing the lid. "This is the best I can do for now, buddy."

He closed the lid and walked back to the driver's side

door. He slid behind the wheel. With the engine running all this time, the snow around the front of the car, including the windshield, had melted considerably which helped him rock back and forth until the car rocketed out of the drifts of snow that had fallen around it. He made a loop around the back yard, using the headlights as spotlights. No sign of anyone else down in the snow. Then he eased along the drive, taking it slower than he wanted to. If he ended up in the ditch he'd be stuck. Every minute wasted was another that could cost Abbey or Hansen.

Who was he kidding? Hansen was likely face down in the snow out in those woods somewhere. Or a hostage to lure Abbey.

Garrett reached Mill Creek Road and managed the necessary turn. He shook his head at the condition of the road. It would be a miracle if he made it to his destination in this vehicle. Three minutes ticked off, each one flickering past on the digital clock on the dash, before he reached the turn to Abbey's house. His frustration ramped higher and higher. It took every ounce of strength he possessed not to floor the accelerator.

As soon as the clearing around the house came into view, he spotted his truck. He shut the headlights off and rolled up behind his vehicle, then killed the engine.

The truck lights were off; engine wasn't running. He edged around the truck, using it as camouflage from the house as he moved closer. The pounding in his chest blocked the sound of the wind. Beyond him, inside the house the silence worried him more than if he'd heard screams.

The tracks from the truck to the house were partially covered but not completely. The tracks he'd made leaving were no longer visible, but these others—the ones of whoever had ambushed him and taken his truck—were still easy enough to see.

Fear tightened around his chest like a vise.

Weapon drawn and ready, he climbed the steps and moved as noiselessly as possible across the dark porch. Still no sound coming from inside. He pressed his back to the wall next to the door and took a moment to steel himself.

If Abbey was already dead—he squeezed his eyes shut and banished the thought. He couldn't be too late.

Like she'd said, there were things they needed to talk about.

With his right hand he reached out and twisted the doorknob. It turned without hesitation. He shoved the door inward and held his ground to the count of three.

No sound. No movement.

He did a one-eighty, stepping into the open doorway.

His gaze moved across the room.

Clear.

No overturned furniture. Nothing broken.

"Abbey!"

His voice echoed in the silence.

More of that choking fear clawed at his throat. He surveyed the room. Scanned the floor for blood. Nothing. His steps as quiet as he could make them, he walked to the kitchen.

"Abbey!" The room was clear. Again, nothing overturned, nothing broken. No blood.

He strode quickly to the staircase, his head throbbing in time with the frantic beating of his heart. He bounded up the stairs. His head swimming after the exertion, he lurched from room to room.

No Abbey.

No sign of a struggle.

Nothing.

Going back down the stairs, he clutched the railing to steady himself. Pain exploded again and again in his head.

His gut roiled and clenched. Couldn't stop. He had to find her.

He stumbled to the kitchen and shoved the curtain aside to stare out the back door. Her SUV was still there. Beyond it was another vehicle. He couldn't see the license plate from the door.

Damn it. Not Hansen's truck.

He considered his options. First, he needed to have another look around outside. The snow had let up considerably. Backup should be here any moment. With two or more deputies they could cover far more ground.

Garrett was at the front door when his cell vibrated. He snatched it from his utility belt hoping against hope it was Abbey.

Coroner.

"Garrett."

"We need to talk about Dottie Hansen."

"You get something back from the lab?" If he had Garrett would be surprised. Most everything that was generally open on a Sunday had shut down early in the afternoon. The lab operated seven days a week, but not in weather conditions like this.

"Believe it or not, I did. Griff Whitley over at the lab couldn't get home—same for me—so he just stayed at work. I asked him to run a tox screen, get me anything possible as quickly as he could, and I proceeded with the autopsy."

"What'd you find?" He needed the man to get straight to the point.

"Either Dottie had decided to take her own life or someone had forced her to swallow a fatal dose of something in the benzodiazepines family. I called Tim Waterman over at the pharmacy and he confirmed that Dottie had been prescribed Valium ages ago. Judging by the surprising lack of blood at the scene, I would say she was almost dead when she was stabbed. Her heart was still beating but barely."

"Why would anyone repeatedly stab a dying woman?" The question was a rhetorical one. In this situation, Garrett knew the answer. Still, it seemed unnecessary for Steven to have forced her to take pills for rendering her immobile and then stabbing her? Why not just put her down the way he had Garrett with that damned baseball bat and then do it?

The scenario introduced a glaring question. Why hadn't he killed Garrett? Why leave him alive?

"Thanks for the update, Doc. I'll get back to you."

His cell vibrated again before he could tuck it back into its holster. *Wagner*.

"Where's that backup?" He needed help here.

"Trees down over the road. The weight of the snow just got to be too much."

What the hell else was going to happen? "You have an ETA for me?"

"Nelson drove back to the Adams' place and borrowed a chainsaw. They'll be through shortly. Should be to your location within the next twenty minutes."

"I'm at the Gray house now. No sign of anyone. No indication there was a struggle of any sort. Whoever put me down, took my truck and drove it here. I had to drive Johnson's patrol car. But I haven't found anyone—alive or otherwise—yet. There is another vehicle behind the house. I'm going to check it out now."

Wagner assured him again that backup would be there soon. Garrett couldn't wait.

He hadn't seen any tracks other than those of his truck out front, so he headed for the back door. He snagged the hat that Abbey's dad had worn everyday off the hook by the door and walked out. If Steven had taken Abbey, they couldn't have gotten far without transportation.

Outside he pulled his flashlight from his utility belt and scanned the snow around Abbey's SUV. Tracks from the far side of the yard had cut across the landscape and ended next to her SUV. Not enough snow on the blue one parked next to hers for it to have been there long. Yellowstone County. Billings was in Yellowstone County and Steven lived in Billings. The make, model and color of the vehicle matched.

Rage fueling him forward, Garrett started a grid pattern, looking for tracks...blood...anything that would give him a direction.

They had to be here...

Somewhere.

More than anything else, he needed her to be alive.

CHAPTER TWELVE

ABBEY DESPERATELY WISHED she'd hidden her cell phone in one of her boots. But she hadn't expected to need to make a move like that. Steven had taken it from her, tossed it into the snow as they started for the tree line.

The strange thing was, she did this sort of thing in her novels. But who believed it would happen to them in real life? Not even her, apparently.

"Keep moving."

This was enough. She stopped. The barrel of the shotgun nudged her in the back. Ignoring the cold steel, she turned around and stared at him. The snow had all but stopped now.

"Why should I?"

Why didn't he just shoot her now and get it over with? Why play this ridiculous game or whatever it was he seemed intent on playing?

He stood close enough for her to see his jaw harden. "When we get to the treehouse, I'll explain everything."

"Why can't you do it now?" She lifted her chin and glared at him. "But first, I want you to take off Garrett's hat. You don't deserve to wear it."

He took a breath, probably to wrangle his frustration. A cloud of cold mist puffed out of his mouth. "When we get to the treehouse, we'll have a good lookout. No one will be able to sneak up on us there. We'll be safe."

She shook her head. "Are you really that stupid?" What did she have to lose at this point? She tapped her temple, baiting him. "Did prison screw you up worse than you already were? Garrett knows about the treehouse. I showed him the evidence you left behind. We both know you've been hiding there. That's the first place he'll look when he comes for you."

Steven shook his head. "This is the only way I can prove the truth to you. I know what I'm doing, Abbey."

If her eyes hadn't adjusted so completely to the dark she might not have seen the plea on his face. The wind had settled allowing her to hear every nuance of his voice. Whether by the grace of insanity or from some piece of goodness that still existed inside him, his words sounded sincere.

"Do you really expect me to believe in you, Steven?"

"I can't make you believe anything you don't want to believe, but I would never have hurt our mother. You must know that's true."

"Why would Mrs. Hansen lie?"

His head moved side to side. "I don't know, but she did and I went to prison for murdering one of the people I loved most in this world. I won't let it happen again."

What did he mean? Let it happen again?

"All right. I'll go with you to the treehouse, but I want you to lower the barrel of that shotgun. You trip and you might end up shooting me whether that's your intent or not."

He lowered the barrel as she'd asked. She turned around and trudged forward. The treehouse wasn't far now. If he was telling the truth and he hadn't arrived until yesterday afternoon, who knocked the ladder down when she was in that treehouse? Who left that food packaging? The pillow and quilt? Why on earth was she allowing herself to trust him again?

Clearly, recent events had sent her over an edge too.

"Just tell me he's okay." She said this without looking back. Wondering if Garrett was okay or not was tearing her heart out.

"He was breathing. I didn't see any blood."

Her chest tightened painfully. Thank God. "Did you hurt him somehow?"

Steven had never been one to fight. He had always walked away or got his butt kicked for trying to walk away. How had that nonviolent guy turned into *this*?

"Here we go," he announced.

They were at the treehouse now. She stared up at the dark façade and wondered if this would be the last thing she saw.

"You go up first."

"You answer my question first. Did you hurt him somehow?"

"I did not. Now go."

An idea occurred to her, making her hesitate. "How can you be sure someone—whoever this mysterious someone is that you believe really killed our mother and Mrs. Hansen— isn't waiting up there for us? Shouldn't the person with the weapon go up first and check it out?"

"Go," he ordered.

He nudged her with the muzzle.

As she climbed the rickety ladder, another thought occurred to her. She smiled to herself. Whatever her brother was doing—whether or not he was telling the truth—she wasn't taking any chances. She had to take control.

To her relief, there was no one waiting in the rickety old former hunting stand to attack her. She scrambled into the treehouse, avoiding the hole she'd made, and eased her way to the far side. The creak of the ladder told her Steven was coming up as promised.

She grabbed one of the little chairs her father had made and readied to do what she had to do to protect herself.

Steven reached the top of the ladder, the barrel of the shotgun pointing skyward. Abbey resisted the impulse to run forward and knock him backward. He was her brother, she didn't want to kill him. She just wanted to stop him from hurting her or anyone else.

He clambered onto the rough wood floor and pushed to his feet.

She rushed forward. Slammed the chair into his left shoulder and his head, sending him staggering to the right, hoping he'd step into the hole and lose his balance.

The chair fell to pieces on the floor. The shotgun hit the floor next. He scrambled to go after it. She charged him.

His fingers went around her throat. He slammed her onto her back on the floor.

"Don't move," he growled in her face. "I swear to God if you do..."

"You'll what? Kill me? Then why bother bringing me here if you were only going to kill me anyway?"

"I'm setting a trap," he snarled as he released her. He retrieved the shotgun and got to his feet. "Get up," he snapped.

She didn't bother. Instead, she crawled to the very back of the space and huddled there. "Talk. Tell me whatever it is you think I need to know about this trap. I want this over."

He stood in the dark silence for a bit. As difficult as it was, she waited.

"Like I said before and during the trial," he began, his voice a low rumble in the night, "I came home from school and found Mom on the ground bleeding. I tried to help her, but it was too late. The next thing I knew Mrs. Hansen was standing there screaming at me. She rushed toward me and pushed me away. She said at the trial that's when she got the blood on her but that's not true. She already had blood on her."

There it was, a repeat of what she had already heard. "Why would anyone believe you now any more than they did back then?" Why was he doing this? "You did your time, Steven? Why would you come back here and do this? You violated your parole leaving Yellowstone County and..." She couldn't say the rest. If he'd killed that old woman to get even. She felt sick.

"I violated the terms of my parole to protect you."

Oh yeah, she'd forgotten that ridiculous plot detail of this ongoing saga. "Did you bring Dad's letter with you?"

"I did."

His answer took her aback. She wasn't expecting that one. Fabric rustled as he dug in his pocket. It was so dark in the treehouse it was hard to tell exactly what he was doing, she could only assume.

"I don't have a flashlight, but here it is." He thrust an envelope at her.

"Well that's convenient." She tucked it into her coat pocket. "I guess I'll have to read it when I get home. Assuming I'm still alive."

He exhaled a big breath. "Dad figured something out. He said so in his letter. He didn't say what but the next day he was dead. That has to tell you something."

"That we are cursed? Have the worst luck? He fell off a ladder, Steven. He wasn't murdered." How did she get that through his head? She shivered as if the cold had only then filtered past the layers of protective wear and absorbed into her bones.

The silence that followed had her hugging her knees to her chest. Had she pushed him too far?

"Dad would never make a mistake like that," he argued. "He'd painted that house numerous times. Done all kinds of maintenance and he never overreached and fell. I think it was made to look that way. There wasn't an autopsy so who knows?"

His words made her uncomfortable. He was right about their father. He'd never fallen before. What if there was some truth to what he was saying?

"Who would have done this?" she demanded, determined not to be swayed without some sort of tangible evidence besides a letter she couldn't read.

"I thought it was Mrs. Hansen at first."

Abbey laughed. "You are kidding, right? The woman wasn't more than five two or five three. She was petite like Mom. How could she have killed a man the size of our father without using a weapon that would leave evidence? You know, like a gun? Not to mention, why in the world would she want to?"

"But," Steven snapped, going on as if she hadn't tossed out a valid loophole in his theory, "when she ended up dead, I knew it was *him*. That's why I rushed home to protect you."

"Who, Steven? Who is *him*?"

"Mr. Hansen."

This was beyond insane. "He's convinced it was you. He looked at me with sheer hatred when I told him how sorry I was to hear about his wife. He was devastated."

"Who else could it have been?"

This was it then. He had no evidence. No idea who did any of this anymore than she did. He'd violated his parole for nothing. He'd done whatever the hell he had done since coming back to town and he had nothing to show for it.

"I'm going to find Garrett."

She was up and at the opening where the ladder waited when he stopped her.

"I can't let you go out there. He'll kill you. We have to wait for him to come to us."

"Why would you want to protect me?" she demanded? "All those years you refused to see us. Returned our letters. Why would you do that and then pretend to come back here to *protect* me like this?"

"I didn't want either of you to be hurt any more than you already had," he said quietly, too quietly. "I didn't want Dad spending any more money on trying to save me when I couldn't be saved."

She wanted to believe him. She really did. But she couldn't.

"I'm going, Steven. If you mean what you say, then you go with me and protect me. Help me prove your story."

He didn't try to stop her as she started down the ladder.

Her feet were on the ground before he started down.

Maybe she could get him back to the house. If Garrett was able, he would be looking for her. *Please let him be okay.*

She backed away from the ladder as Steven lowered his feet to the ground.

A cold, gloved hand grabbed her by the throat and yanked her backward.

She yelped.

A muzzle pressed into her temple.

Steven spun around, the barrel of the shotgun leveled in front of him. "What took you so long?"

A new kind of fear lit inside Abbey. Was her brother working with a partner?

"Put it down!" the man holding her commanded.

Time seemed to stop for a moment as her brain digested and recognized the raised voice.

Lionel Hansen.

This couldn't be right. He had always been like family.

No, she realized, Steven was family. Hansen was just the man next door who had a gun aimed at her head.

As if he'd sensed a new tension in her body, Hansen jerked her closer against him. "Put it down or she's dead."

Steven tossed the shotgun to the snow-covered ground.

"You're not taking anyone else from me," her brother warned.

Hansen laughed, the sound evil and twisted. "You won't miss her because you'll be dead too."

Abbey rode out the wave of new shock. She inhaled sharply. She had to do something.

"Garrett is on his way," she lied. "He'll be here any minute."

Another vicious laugh. "And when he arrives, he'll find that your crazy brother has killed you and then himself."

Terror twisted inside Abbey even as a sobering realization overtook her. "He's telling the truth, isn't he?"

"You of all people should know the truth can be whatever you want it to be," Hansen countered. "Sometimes the story changes and you have to revise."

Anger erupted inside her. "You killed our parents!"

"No."

The old man uttered the single syllable with a mixture of agony and anger.

Maybe if she distracted him, he would loosen his grip on her or lower his weapon. It was worth a shot. "I don't believe you."

"I loved her."

More of that anguish weighted his angry words.

"But you killed her anyway," Abbey said, improvising.

Steven was staring at her. She couldn't tell what he was thinking but she hoped he understood her goal.

"I would never have hurt her. Never." Hansen shook his head adamantly. Abbey felt the movement. "I would have done anything for Ellen. She was the love of my life. My heart."

Another unexpected quake rocked through Abbey. She wished she could see Steven's expression more clearly. Had he known this too?

"But she didn't love you," her brother said. "She loved our father. She would never have looked at anyone else."

"He was nothing but an obstacle," Hansen sneered. "I would have found a way and the opportunity one day to clear my path. I could wait. I would have waited the rest of my life, content to see her from time to time. Hear her voice. Relish her occasional touch when her hand accidentally brushed mine."

His words turned her stomach. "But you decided you couldn't, and you killed her instead," Abbey suggested, following Steven's lead. "If you couldn't have her, no one could."

His hand clamped harder around her throat, making her gag.

"*She* killed her."

Abbey froze, the pressure on her throat no longer important.

"Your wife killed my mother?" The words were hers, but she didn't recognize them. Whether from the shock or from the grip on her throat.

"She was jealous. She knew how I felt. I tried to hide it, but it was impossible."

Steven stepped forward.

The muzzle of the weapon Hansen held bored deeper into Abbey's skull.

"You knew it was her and you let me go to jail for it?"

"I was devastated. I couldn't think straight for months,"

Hansen argued. "Dottie was all I had left. I couldn't lose her too. Anything was better than being alone."

Steven called him every vile name in his vocabulary. The more he shouted, the faster the man holding Abbey breathed as if the ugly words were pushing the oxygen from his lungs faster than he could fill them. The rasp of his respiration brushed against her hair. He was shaken to the core.

Good.

"That was a long time ago," Abbey said, cutting off her brother's rampage and redirecting the conversation. "Why kill her now? She was still all you had. Aren't you going to be lonely without her?"

"It was the dementia. The confusion started a little over a year ago. She couldn't remember things that happened five minutes before. It was as if the past was her five minutes ago. She kept getting confused. She said something to your father that had him demanding answers from me about Ellen. I knew he'd just keep digging until he figured out how much I had loved her and what happened when she died. I had no choice but to kill him."

Abbey's knees almost buckled. She steadied herself, struggled to keep the discussion going. "Garrett said he fell off a ladder. He would never lie to me." This man had to be lying.

"I made it look that way. The deputy who showed up was completely convinced. Problem solved. He's dead now too so that's that."

White hot rage blasted against her chest. Before she could scream at him all the hateful names that came to her mind, he went on, "Dottie just kept getting worse. The more the disease dragged her into the past, the bigger liability she became to me. When I found out you were coming back to pack up the house, I decided to do what had to be done. It was perfect timing. I knew Garrett would find some way to blame Steven for yours and Dottie's murders. So, I took that bat from his room. I was going to beat her to death with it when I got home and say I found her that way except she beat me to the punch. But like everything else she did in her life, she was never quite thorough enough."

Revulsion roiled through her. Abbey warned, "Garrett won't be fooled by any of this."

"That's right," Steven piped up, taking another step toward them, "he's not like that good old boy sheriff we had when our mother was killed. He won't stop until he finds the truth."

"Stop right there," Hansen ordered. He shrugged his left shoulder, then passed the gun to his left hand and shrugged his right shoulder. Something fell to the ground. "There's a rope in that pack. Fix yourself a hanging noose, Steven. Today's the day you're going to end your suffering. I'll let you go first so you don't have to watch your sister die. Whatever you think, I'm not completely heartless."

"I won't let you hurt her," Steven argued, moving yet another step toward them.

"You can't stop me," Hansen warned. "I've planned everything out. In this weather it'll be hard to tell who went first. Course I'll make sure the weapon has your prints on it and your hand has powder burns. I've watched enough CSI reruns to know what I have to do. As good as Garrett Gilmore is, he won't figure it out. He'll be too devastated that he couldn't stop this tragedy."

It was now or never. Abbey relaxed her body to give him a false sense of control. "Go ahead, Steven," she urged. "There's no point fighting the inevitable. You go first. I'll be right behind you."

He stared at her.

Did he not understand? "Do it," she shouted. "Now!"

As if he'd only then realized what she meant, he darted past her and Hansen. Disappeared in the darkness.

"Stop you son of—" Hansen instinctively shifted his aim toward her fleeing brother.

Abbey jerked out of his hold, whipped around and pushed him as hard as she could, sending him face forward into the snow.

She took off in the direction her brother had disappeared. She zigzagged around and between the trees, praying she wouldn't run headlong into one.

Hansen's shouted warnings echoed through the trees.

She kept going.

A gunshot rang out in the darkness.

CHAPTER THIRTEEN

Backup had arrived.

Garrett sent Nelson and Tracey to look around the Hansen place in hopes of finding the old man and to start securing the scene. Two deputies had transferred Johnson's body to a body bag and then into the back of a department SUV for Deputy Cunningham to transport to the morgue. Since Johnson was a widower and didn't have any children or known next of kin, there was no one to notify. His family was the department and they would take care of his final arrangements when this storm was done so they could do it right.

Garrett and the other three deputies had spread out to begin a grid search of the woods surrounding Abbey's home. The longer she was out in this weather the less likely she could survive. He didn't want to find any more bodies.

He couldn't bear the idea of her...

Shake it off. Don't go down that road.

Garrett was a dozen yards into the tree line when he heard the gunshot.

The beam of his flashlight guiding him, he ran toward the blast. The others fanned out and did the same. Garrett's movements were stilted and unstable, but whatever his injury it could wait. He had to find Abbey.

Before it was too late.

He ran harder. His right shoulder banked off a tree. He grimaced but kept going. With the overhead canopy of evergreens, the snow wasn't as deep this far into the woods. Made moving forward considerably less difficult. Didn't slow the throbbing in his head. He kept going. Unless his body quit on him, he wouldn't stop.

He spotted movement to his left. Whoever it was, he didn't have a flashlight. Wouldn't be one of his deputies. They all had flashlights and wore the department jackets with reflective lettering.

Garrett pushed forward, ignoring the pain that continued to rip through his skull.

When he was within a few yards of the fleeing figure, whoever the hell it was suddenly stopped and started yelling and waving his arms frantically.

"He took her! He's going to kill her!"

Male. Strained, hoarse voice.

Garrett caught up to him and grabbed him by the coat. *Lionel Hansen.* "Who took her?" he demanded.

Hansen gasped for breath. "Steven...that murdering brother of hers. He's taking her to the river, going to kill her." He shook his head and started to wail hysterically, his words not making sense.

"Are you injured?" Garrett demanded.

Hansen trembled uncontrollably whether from fear or merely the cold Garrett couldn't be sure. "Are you injured?" he repeated, needing him to pay attention. There was no time...

Hansen's head wagged side to side. "No. No. You have to go save her. He's got a gun!"

Deputy Carla Vincent joined the huddle. "I've got him, Sheriff."

"Take him to the house. Get him warmed up and take his statement."

"Yes, sir."

Garrett headed for the river that cut across the properties on this side of Mill Creek Road. His heart pounded faster and faster. If Steven was armed and had made his intentions known, Garrett might have no other choice but to take him down.

Bottom line, for now she was alive and he had to make sure she stayed that way.

Movement in the distance on his right snagged his attention.

A flash of light against darkness.

Not a flashlight. Not reflective lettering.

White coat.

Abbey.

He restrained the urge to call out to her. If she'd evaded Steven, he didn't want to give away her position.

Garrett pushed his body harder, lunged through the trees in that direction. If he could catch up with Abbey before Steven got her back in his crosshairs, he might be able to avoid a violent confrontation.

Snow crunched.

To his left.

Another figure rushing in the same direction as Abbey whizzed past his line of sight.

Had to be Steven.

Garrett altered his course to intersect with his new target.

The one nearest him glanced back.

Tall. Had to be Steven.

Garrett charged forward.

A scream split the air.

Abbey.

"Stay right there, Garrett!"

He stopped, almost went face down in the snow with the effort. Garrett kept his weapon lowered. He didn't want to make the man feel more threatened than he already did...*yet.* "Let her go, Steven, and we'll figure this out."

Garrett strained to see the weapon...not visible.

He laughed. "If I let her go, you'll end up shooting me and then they'll win. Again."

"Listen to him, Garrett," Abbey urged. "You're not thinking clearly or you wouldn't be doing this."

Garrett couldn't see her eyes or her face well enough to read her emotional state, but he trusted her. "I won't shoot you, Steven," he assured him. "You have my word."

The whisper of snow packing sounded behind him. Garrett didn't have to look back to know it was his two deputies. A new wave of tension rippled through him. Their arrival would make the man more nervous.

"Tell them to stay back," Steven cautioned, his voice calmer than Garrett had expected.

"Garrett, please," Abbey urged, "you have to listen to him. He's telling the truth."

"Hold your position," Garrett ordered his deputies. He shifted his attention to the man holding so tight to Abbey. "You don't need Abbey to protect you. I won't allow this situation to go wrong."

"The last sheriff I trusted caused me to spend nearly half my life in prison."

Abbey pulled free of her brother's hold.

Garrett braced to launch himself between her and the other man.

"Wait! Garrett, wait." Abbey held up her hands. Rather than run, she stood in front of Steven as if attempting to shield him.

"I'll hear him out," Garrett promised her. "Just let me do this the right way." Damn it! She needed to move aside.

"It's not Steven," she cried. "It never was. Hansen is the one." A sob tore past her lips. "Steven has been telling the truth all along."

Garrett holstered his weapon. Held up his hands and glanced over one shoulder then the other. "Lower your weapons."

The two deputies did as he ordered but not without a moment's hesitation. He wouldn't have expected less.

Taking a deep breath and hoping like hell he wasn't making a mistake, Garrett turned back to Steven. "Put your weapon down and we'll figure this out."

Abbey looked back at her brother, said something Garrett couldn't make out. Every second ticked off like a bomb exploding inside him. Somewhere on the perimeter of his consciousness he was aware his head still throbbed, but he ignored it.

Steven held up his hands. "I don't have a weapon. We left the shotgun back at the treehouse."

"He's telling the truth," Abbey said to Garrett. Then to her brother, she urged, "You can trust him." She turned to Garrett and started toward him.

Garrett held his breath until she was close enough for him to hug her. "You sure about this?"

She nodded, drew back. "Hansen was going to kill us back there. He killed our father."

Garrett didn't have to question her about the statement. If she said it, she was certain it was accurate. A new kind of outrage tore through him. "Mitchell," he called to the deputy on his right, "Get these two safely back to the house." He turned to the one on his left. "Come with me, Prater."

"Be careful, Garrett," Abbey called behind him, "he has a handgun."

Garrett held her gaze a moment longer. He barely restrained the urge to hug her again. Instead, he nodded, then took off through the trees.

He had never known Lionel Hansen to own a handgun. A rifle, a shotgun, yes. If he was armed with a handgun, then he'd taken it from someone.

Like Deputy Johnson.

Wherever the adrenaline came from Garrett was thankful for it. He made it to the tree line in record time. Prater right behind him.

The first thing he spotted was only two of the three SUVs that should have been parked in front of the house.

One was gone.

The second thing was the tan uniform in the snow.

Fury propelled another burst of adrenaline into his veins.

Garrett rushed to the side of the downed deputy and checked the carotid pulse as Prater called for emergency medical aid.

Still alive.

Thank God.

One shot. Lower torso.

Garrett lifted Carla Vincent into his arms and struggled through the snow to the house. When he settled her on the kitchen table he turned to Prater. "Take care of her. I'm going after Hansen."

Prater was already removing Vincent's coat. "I got this. Be careful, Sheriff. That old man seems determined to take as many as possible with him before he goes down."

Garrett gave his deputy a nod.

He was in the SUV and turning around when he spotted Abbey, her brother and his deputy emerging from the tree line.

At least that was something to be grateful for in this damned mess.

He barreled down the drive, following in the tracks rutted out. Thank God the snow had slowed to a near stop. He radioed dispatch and put out an APB on Hansen and the missing department vehicle.

He'd barely tossed aside the mike and powered the windows down to look both ways on Mill Creek when the missing SUV came into view.

Garrett eased out of the drive, going right. The SUV sat in the middle of the road, brake lights glaring. He rolled to a stop in the rutted snow behind the SUV. He jumped out, weapon drawn and approached the driver's side with caution. A murdered deputy, a murdered elderly woman.

He killed our father.

Whatever Hansen was doing, he hadn't moved. Brakes were still engaged.

Maybe he had another story to tell about what happened to his wife. To one of Garrett's finest.

Besides Abbey's father, who else had this SOB murdered?

Rage roaring through him, Garrett jerked the driver's side door open and shoved the muzzle of his weapon into the driver's face.

Lionel Hansen turned his head, his hand pressed to his abdomen, blood oozing from between his fingers.

As much as Garrett wanted to let him die, he called it in and did what he could to help until EMA arrived.

CHAPTER FOURTEEN

Noon

ABBEY WAITED in Garrett's office. She had never been so exhausted, grateful, hurt and angry in her life. All those years of pain and disappointment she and her family had suffered had been for naught.

Steven was innocent.

Garrett had interviewed and taken a statement from her and Steven separately. She hadn't taken offense. From her book research, she understood this was standard protocol. He and Deputy Sheriff Wagner were at the hospital interviewing Hansen. They'd had to wait until after his surgery.

She wasn't sure she would feel warm and rested again until she'd had a long, hot bath and about a hundred hours of sleep.

The door opened and she looked up, expecting Garrett with news. Not Garrett. Steven.

She smiled. Her brother looked as rattled and unkempt as she had when she'd finally had a chance to seek asylum in the ladies' room. "You okay?" she asked.

He sat down in the chair beside her and appeared to think about the question for a moment. "Yeah. I think so. I'll let you know when all the shock wears off."

"I understand."

With the polite conversation out of the way, they sat together in silence for a while. She imagined he felt as exhausted and emotionally rattled as she did. Maybe more so. Nearly half his life had been stolen from him. She desperately wished she could change that tragedy, but she could not. There were, however, some things she could do.

"I was thinking," she said. She studied his face, so familiar and yet so alien to her. She hadn't seen him in person in sixteen years. His jaw was leaner, more square now. His shoulders had broadened and his tall lanky frame had filled out. No matter that his voice was much deeper, she still heard nuances of the teenage brother she'd adored in there somewhere. "We should go ahead with selling the place. You take the money and buy you a home and whatever else you need. Daddy would want you to have it. You've paid too much for the mistakes of others to be faced with unnecessary stress and compromise in the future. I don't want you suffering financially or any other way from this point forward."

He stared at her for a long time before he spoke. "That wouldn't be right. What happened wasn't your fault. You shouldn't be trying to shoulder the burden of making it right. It happened. We can't change history."

"I don't need the money, Steven. My career is doing great. I'm good. I want you to go to college or whatever it is you want to do. You deserve happiness. I want you to see your future with whatever vision feels right."

He laughed, a soft, low sound. "I'm thankful the truth has finally come out, but I missed a lot, Sis. I can't get that back. Money, college, none of that really matters."

She understood he meant the time with their father. "He

talked about you all the time, you know. He always said things like, when Steven can come home. When Steven this or that. You might not have been here, but you were always in his thoughts—in our thoughts."

"Thank you." He lowered his head. "Knowing that means a great deal to me."

"You should come visit me in New York. I have a pretty cool apartment."

He searched her eyes for another of those long moments. "Are you sure you want to go back to New York?"

She made a face. "Of course. Why would you ask?" Guilt that maybe he thought she should hang around a while for him instantly plagued her. "I can stay a while, if you'd like. I really could use your help going through things at the house."

He laughed out loud this time. "Not for me or all that," he said. "For you and Garrett."

Before she could stop it, heat rushed up her throat. "We're friends, Steven. Like always, but—"

Steven shook head. "I've seen the way he looks at you. I saw it when we were kids. The guy has spent his whole life in love with you. How can you not see that?"

Before she was forced to respond, the door opened again. This time it was Garrett. He closed the door behind him and rounded his desk, then collapsed into his chair. "This has been a long day."

Abbey couldn't help herself, she stared at him. As disheveled as he was, he looked amazing. Handsome, sexy, strong. Her heart did the wildest little flip flop.

"Really long," Steven agreed, looking from Garrett to her.

She blinked and quickly nodded. "Do we know anything more about why Mr. Hansen did..." Emotion clogged her throat. She didn't need to say the rest, both knew what she meant.

"Once he conferred with his attorney, he told me every-thing—at least he claimed it was everything."

Abbey chewed her lip as she waited for Garrett to explain.

Steven didn't wait. "Did he kill her? Our mother, I mean?"

"According to him, that was his wife."

"I knew it." Steven shook his head. "I tried to tell everyone that Mrs. Hansen already had blood all over her when I found Mom. But no one would listen to me. They took her word over mine."

"Why?" Abbey needed to understand what had motivated the Hansens to hurt her family. They'd been neighbors all those years. Friends, for God's sake. Holiday dinners, church outings. They'd done so many things together before...that awful day.

"Hansen says he was in love with your mother—not that she ever did anything to make him feel that way," Garrett explained. "He was the first to say she was completely inno-cent of his obsession."

"He told us that in the woods, but it's still difficult to believe." Abbey turned to Steven. "Did you ever see any indi-cation of this?" She'd been too young to notice. Or maybe Hansen had been careful around her.

Steven slowly nodded. "Yeah, I think I did. He watched Mom whenever he was around. You know, really watched her. He was always bringing her gifts he claimed were from his wife. I always wondered why Mrs. Hansen didn't bring the gifts. But I was a stupid teenager, I never made the connec-tion. I was too absorbed in my own dramas."

"He claimed," she said to Garrett then, "that he covered for his wife so he wouldn't be alone." She shook her head. "But if he'd really loved our mother, he would have wanted justice for her." Abbey drew in a deep breath to calm herself. The man was obviously warped or otherwise mentally impaired. "This was never about love. It was about obsession."

"He claimed he didn't want anyone to find out about his obsession with her," Garrett told them. "His wife threatened to tell everything if he didn't protect her, so he did. He claims he was actually protecting your mother from any gossip or rumors. He said he wanted to protect her too."

"Did he tell you that she had dementia?" Steven asked. "He claims she said something to Dad which is what got him killed. He confronted Hansen about whatever it was and well, you know the rest."

Abbey suddenly remembered the letter. Where was her coat? She looked around, spotted it on the floor next to her chair. She reached down and pulled the letter from her coat pocket. She leaned forward and thrust the wrinkled envelope across the desk. "He sent Steven this letter but by the time he received it, it was too late. That is evidence—proof of what Steven is telling you."

Steven met her gaze. She saw the appreciation in his eyes that she had given the letter to Garrett without even opening it. Because she trusted her brother. He had never been a liar much less a killer.

Garrett read the letter and placed it on his desk. "Thank you. This will be useful in the event Hansen attempts to withdraw his confession."

"Can he do that?" Steven wanted to know.

Abbey was aware of some option along those lines, but she wasn't versed enough in the law to respond. Surely it wasn't as simple as him changing his mind.

"He can try but it wouldn't be easy. He made his confession freely with his attorney present. About the only way it could be thrown out is if the attorney was able to prove he wasn't mentally fit to say the things he said." Garrett looked to Abbey. "Based on all he said, I'm reasonably confident he used your arrival as the opportunity to set his wife's death as well as yours in motion. He stole Steven's bat from his room to try and implicate him."

Abbey's breath hitched. "I see his motive for wanting to kill his wife. He couldn't trust her not to say the wrong thing anymore, but why would he have wanted to kill me or Steven?"

"To make it appear Steven came back and finished off everyone involved."

"I can't believe the man I knew all those years was so evil." Abbey shook her head.

"I can," Steven admitted. "I saw it all in prison. You never know a person until you've shared time with them up close and personal."

Something else Abbey deeply regretted.

"Mrs. Hansen understood her problem as well," Garrett went on to explain. "She went to your house that day, before you arrived. She took your mother's pearls and the lipstick she wore all the time as well as one of her dresses. Rather than wait for her husband to decide she was too much of a liability, she chose to go the suicide route. I suppose as a jab to him, she dressed herself up like your mother before taking an entire bottle of the Valium she'd been prescribed. Then she waited for him to come home."

"So he didn't kill her?" Abbey felt confused. Hansen had said something like she beat him to the punch. Obviously, she was too tired to be following. Maybe she needed more coffee...or sleep.

"He finished her off," Garrett clarified. "She expected to be dead by the time he arrived, but I guess she overestimated the dosage she'd ingested. She was still breathing when Hansen found her. He arranged the crime scene to look as if Steven had returned and done the deed. What she'd done startled him so that he forgot about the bat and used a knife."

Garrett grimaced. "I have the concussion to prove he remembered the bat later, however."

"They checked you out at the hospital while you were waiting for Hansen to come out of surgery?" Abbey had hoped he wouldn't ignore his own injury.

"They did." Garrett looked from her to Steven and back. "In the end, Hansen had decided that if he killed everyone related to your mother's death, the past would never be resurrected."

Abbey shook herself to clear the awful images from her mind. "What about Mom's pearls? Were they with Mrs. Hansen's body?"

"Hansen took them intending to keep them as a memento of your mother."

"What about the stuff in the treehouse?" Steven asked. "Who was staying there? It damned sure wasn't me."

"It was a hunter. He thought I was with Fish & Wildlife when I dropped by the Munford place. When the APB went out for you, we mentioned a potential sighting in that area," Garrett explained, "the guy called in and said he was the one. He didn't want us chasing our tails when a suspected murderer was running around."

Steven nodded.

"Sounds like all the loose ends are tied up." Abbey was greatly relieved. The sooner this nightmare was over, the happier she would be. She had every intention of ensuring the local newspapers ran front page stories about her brother's innocence.

"Just about," Garrett agreed.

His gaze lingered on her and her heart reacted to what she saw in his.

"I need a shower and food." Steven stood as if keenly aware they needed a minute.

Garrett pushed to his feet and extended his hand. "Thank you for what you did to protect Abbey."

Steven shook his hand, then shrugged. "I'm surprised you're not detaining me since I violated my parole coming here."

"I've already cleared that up. It'll take a bit of paperwork, but all that is going away. The state of Montana will be talking to you about compensation. What happened to you was wrong. We have to make that as close to right as possible."

Abbey couldn't help herself. She shot to her feet, grabbed her brother and hugged him hard. They both cried just a little. Happy tears this time.

"Deputy Nelson will take you to the Murray. There's a room and an unlimited bar and dining tab waiting for you there."

When Steven had gone, Abbey stood very still, waiting to see what would happen next. Steven was right about more than who killed their mother. It was time, she and Garrett figured out this thing between them.

"Your place will be a crime scene for a few days." Garrett shrugged, the movement as weary as she felt. "The storm is moving out. Wyoming and Colorado are bracing for the worst and we'll be cleaning up. I'm grateful it's behind us for the most part. I guess we can get on with the rest of our lives now."

"Still no storm-related fatalities in our county?" she queried trying to keep her voice even, her tone light.

"None that we know of. There could be folks in those mountain cabins who didn't make it. But we can hope we survived without any lives lost. I will be immensely grateful if we do."

She could leave now and his life could go back to normal.

Maybe that pretty reporter, Camille whatever her name was, would finally get the guy.

Deep inside, an ache pierced her.

No.

She wanted this guy.

"Right." She reached down for her coat. "I'll be around for a couple weeks more." She shrugged. "I guess I'll be at the Murray too."

He skirted his desk and took her coat, tossed it onto the chair Steven had vacated. "Actually, I was hoping you'd stay at the ranch for a while. You have that book to finish and the roads will be a mess for days. No need for you to rush. Steven can do the packing up. He needs some time to adjust without a lot of outside interference. Spending time at the house alone will be good for him."

Abbey peered into those dark eyes she knew so well. "Good points. But why would you want me to stay with you? Something like this could damage your bachelor status."

He grinned. "Being a bachelor isn't all it's cracked up to be."

"I see." She nodded. "You want me to help relieve you of that problem?"

"Abbey." He cupped her face in his hands. "If I could have married you at fourteen, I would have."

"We were foolish kids," she argued no matter that her heart was racing so she could hardly manage a breath.

"I have never wanted to spend my life with anyone else. I should have told you this years ago, but I was afraid you didn't feel the same way. Maybe you don't now, but it feels like you do. If I'm misreading the signs, set me straight and we'll leave it at that."

"Apparently we've been in the same boat all these years," she said. "We just didn't know it. But we know it now. I really want to give *us* a try, Garrett. We can work out the logistics later."

He tilted her face up to meet his and kissed her. Softly at first, then with all the passion she felt simmering inside him. Inside herself.

Holly had passed, but this was just the beginning of a new kind of storm—one of sweet emotions and endless possibilities.

LIVINGSTON 31 NEWS

The cameraman gave Camille the countdown and then she was live with her final on-location broadcast about Winter Storm Holly.

"I have good news today, folks. We survived Holly! Perfect timing for the start of the work week. Holly is passing over northern Wyoming and barreling toward Colorado. Portal, near Denver, is dead in her path. If you have friends or family in that area, urge them to take care. Rather than winding down, Holly hasn't stopped building momentum since she started. Colorado may see her worst yet. Thankfully here, in our viewing area, we can move on to preparing for the holidays. There are only nine days until Christmas, folks. It's time to get back in the spirit."

Camille smiled broadly for the camera. "Thanks again to all those deputies and police officers and so many other emergency personnel who helped us get through this record-breaking storm. This is Camille Dutton, Channel 31 News. Back to the studio!"

Thanks for reading! If you enjoyed this book, please do leave a review.

Read on for a sneak peek of the next STORM WATCH novel, *Deep Freeze* by Vicki Hinze.

SNEAK PEEK

DEEP FREEZE
STORMWATCH, Book 2
by Vicki Hinze
Copyright © 2019 by Vicki Hinze

Tuesday, December 17th

Darcy Keller stood on the side of the road in the blowing snow and checked her earpiece, watching for her cameraman's cue. He counted down the last three seconds on his fingers. The anchor at the station segued to Darcy for the live shot.

"A severe weather alert has been issued for our viewing area. Holly is the worst storm in eighty years, and she's earning the title," Darcy began. "Fatalities and extensive damage are being reported in Montana.

"This morning, an abrupt jog has turned the storm to Colorado. Specifically, onto you, Portal. The weather is deteriorating rapidly. As you can see behind me, whiteout conditions are already occurring. High winds and a mix of snow and ice are making travel extremely dangerous and next to impossible. Authorities are advising you get where you're going now and settle in.

"For the last several hours, flights have been halted in Denver and diverted to Portal International Airport. We're about five miles from PIA now, and it's taken hours to get this far. All along our path, we've witnessed cars spinning and sliding off the road. An eighteen-wheeler jack-knifed near the intersection of Interstates 25 and 76. The driver is critically injured. Stranded motorists have abandoned their vehicles and are seeking shelter on foot despite being warned to stay with their vehicles. Temperatures are plummeting. We expect subzero within the hour. Roads are closed to all but emergency vehicles and will remain shut down until after the storm passes. The National Guard has been activated to assist stranded drivers but, be warned, if the winds get much higher, they, too, will be sidelined, as will emergency responders.

"Over 1800 flights have been canceled at DIA in Denver. Now, I've just been advised, the diversionary airport in Portal has closed. With over 5,000 stranded travelers, Portal International is well over capacity. Our crew has been trying to make the typically thirty-minute trek from the station to PIA for over two and a half hours.

"At the moment, authorities are uncertain how many are

without power, though they expect the number will be extraordinarily high by tomorrow morning due to ice and near hurricane-strength winds.

"We'll be on-site at PIA—Portal International—with live updates as soon as possible. Authorities urge residents to exercise extreme caution. In all of Portal's recorded history, we have not seen a storm like this. It's critical to your safety and your family's that you listen to the authorities. Follow their advice. Hunker down, Portal. And stay tuned for the latest weather alerts.

"A personal observation: Conditions are already rough out here. They are going to get a lot worse before they get better. Avoid taking risks, check your emergency supplies, and stay safe. Remember, things can be replaced. You can't.

"This is Darcy Keller for Portal 3 News. Back to you in the studio…"

Chapter One
1440 (2:40 PM)

Why do weathermen and women stand outside in near hurricane-strength winds, blowing snow and ice, to relay Emergency Weather Alerts, reporting dangerous weather conditions, and urge residents to stay indoors?

Emma Miller stood in a cluster of stranded travelers staring up at the TV screen in the Portal Airport terminal unable to think of one good reason for a person to put themselves through that misery. From Darcy Keller's involuntary twitches, the ice pelting her stung through her heavy red coat and the hood covering her head. Worse, she was clearly pregnant. A couple standing near Emma questioned the wisdom of Darcy Keller being out in the storm, risking a fall or injury.

Silently, Emma agreed. The ice was slick. The heavy scarf at Darcy's neck draped down the front of her coat, and she wore a hood and gloves and boots so the only exposed skin was on her face, yet the cold air fogged her breath to the point viewers couldn't clearly make out her features.

From the advisory, it didn't appear Emma or any of the other passengers diverted from Denver to Portal were going anywhere anytime soon. Figured. At least the plane had landed before the airport shut down.

Emma had been exhausted before getting on the plane, though the adrenaline rush had gotten her this far on the long flight. When taxiing in, she had spotted a hotel attached to the last terminal by a long breezeway, but odds were it was already booked or there wouldn't be so many people staking out sections of floor in the airport terminal itself. Every seat was taken and most of the floor, too.

She searched her jacket pockets. Found her phone and half a tin of cinnamon Altoids. No purse, no money, nothing but the clothes on her back and the ticket and ID she'd had the foresight to stash in her slacks' pocket before making the rescue attempt. Darcy Keller had been right. It was going to be a rough couple of days.

Emma walked on from the gate area, looking for a less populated spot with at least semi-privacy to phone in a report to Home Base. The second terminal was as crowded as the third had been, and the first, Terminal A, was even worse than B or C. The din of voices droned a constant hum that hung in the air. She pressed on to the northern end of an area identified by signs as "the Main." It was a broad and expansive opening defined by overhead, tented awnings, a food court and clusters of shops. Midway through it, she spotted a blessedly empty alcove and ducked into it, then retrieved her phone and contacted Home Base.

"Silencers. Liz speaking. How may I direct your call?"

Seeing the young redhead in her mind, Emma spoke softly. "Liz, it's Emma." Why was the Director of Operations answering the phone rather than the receptionist, Billie?

"Are you on the ground?"

"Yes, but not in Denver."

"They diverted you to Portal, correct?"

"Yes. And as soon as we were wheels down and landed, they shut the airport." Emma scanned the crowd rushing the food court. "Any chance you can get me some transportation out of—"

"None," Liz said, cutting her off. "You've been diverted."

Spotting an older silver-haired man with a thick briefcase and stooped shoulders, Emma visually followed him from an outlying sportswear store to the food court. Definitely browsing. "We've established that, Liz."

"I don't mean the flight. I mean, we—Silencers—have diverted you."

Surprise streaked through Emma. They were reassigning her to another security detail assignment already? She hadn't yet gotten home from the last one, and it had been grueling. Hostage rescue operations were always rough. "To where?"

"You're there. Portal International Airport."

"Seriously?" More perplexed than anything else, Emma inhaled deeply and caught the scent of lemon. She looked up and sure enough, there was a vent overhead. Why anyone, especially in an airport, would mask scents, she had no idea. It was a prime violation of protocol and an opportunity for unsavory types to insert bio-contaminates.

"Seriously," Liz said. "Look at it this way. You're stuck there anyway. At least you'll be busy during the storm."

"There are thousands of people crammed into this facility, Liz. Surely PIA has its own security team." Every international airport did these days.

"It does," she agreed. "But your assignment isn't to secure the facility or the people."

That disclosure made Emma's mission as clear as mud. Briefcase Man reappeared with coffee and a pretzel. "What am I securing then?" Emma couldn't imagine.

"Just let me tell you, okay? I'm slammed here today— Billie is out until God knows when with the flu—so I need to streamline for efficiency."

Emma didn't sigh. She wanted to, but she didn't. "Fine. Go ahead."

"Use your same cover. Investigative journalist for American National Reporters—and no Loeb Award nominations this time. The director is still freaking out over the notoriety on your first mission."

Emma nearly had been booted from Silencers' training program over that. Security Specialists were most effective if forgettable and unnoticed. According to Liz, Emma's looks were Strike One against her. The award nomination, a huge Strike Two. If she got a Third Strike, she would be kicked out of the program. It was that simple. Everything she'd been working toward these past three years would be gone in a snap. No discussion. No reprieve. And no exceptions. Her fingers curled tightly around the phone. "I understand."

"Stay put under the tent in The Main. That's an area with stretched canvas overhead in the main terminal."

She'd seen the signs. "I'm there now."

"Good." Liz sounded relieved further explanation was unnecessary. "Apparently, a lot of construction's going on there."

"Noted that on the way in. Looks especially comprehensive on Levels Three and Four."

"It is, or so we're told. Heavy renovations. Fortunately, you'll be located elsewhere in the facility, so it shouldn't be an issue."

Regardless of where you were located in the facility, those open construction areas created worrisome vulnerabilities. Emma refrained from saying so.

"Your point of contact will retrieve you in fifteen minutes. Six-two, one-ninety, blue eyes, hasn't shaved in a few days, but he's a good-looking guy. His name is Dr. Gregory Martin."

Checking her watch beneath her black coat sleeve, Emma stilled. "Dr. Gregory Mason Martin?" Her throat thick, she waited for Liz's response. Dread churned with curiosity in her stomach.

"Yes, that's him."

A shiver coursed up Emma's backbone. Of all the people in the world, why him? The entire mission just wrapped up had been like this. She hadn't been able to catch a break with both hands and a net.

"Bio-containment expert. He runs the high-containment facility there that only a few know exists."

Emma frowned into her phone. "There's a high-containment lab here, in this airport?" What genius did that? Airports being terrorist targets had required they be hardened, but, good grief. Bio-contaminates in an airport? That was just insane.

"Afraid so."

Stranded in a wicked storm in a facility under heavy construction. Five thousand souls at stake, and now this. Bio-contaminates *and* Mason Martin. The news tumbled straight through bad and into worse. If not to protect the facility or people, why was she being diverted? "What's my job here?"

"Keep the lab secure," Liz said, then dropped her voice. "You know this doctor, correct?"

Another shiver coursed through Emma. "I do, yes."

"From a prior mission?" Liz asked, though she knew the answer already. Liz never asked a question she couldn't already answer.

"Actually, no. We grew up together and went to the same college. He knows me, Liz. My cover isn't going—"

"It will hold as much as is needed. His headquarters will see to it. This acquaintance could be helpful. If the doctor knows you, he is less apt to expose you."

"That's an assumption." Emma frowned. "He may be more apt."

"Oh, boy."

"What?" The scent changed to cinnamon rolls. She sniffed. Coming from the vent.

"That change in your tone. I only hear it when something is personal." Liz hesitated but when Emma remained silent, she added, "Were you engaged to him?"

Naturally, that'd be the first thing to occur to Liz. "No."

"Ah, so he must be the one who got away."

Surprise rippled across Emma's chest. "How do you know one got away?"

"Reasonable deduction. Anytime we talk about relationships, it's written all over your face," Liz said. "More accurately, it appears whenever we talk about the breakup of another of your relationships."

Emma clamped her jaw shut. Okay, so she'd been engaged a few times and had never made it to the altar. So what? Wasn't that better than a string of divorces? She opened her mouth to fire back a snarky retort, but fortunately good sense intervened. If she wanted to get out of training and off probation and be permanently hired at Silencers, Inc., the last thing she needed to do was to cross Liz and lose her support. "No, he isn't the one who got away." Oh, Emma hated admitting this. "Speaking honestly, he's the one I never got."

"I see." Liz's tone held empathy, proving she did see. Too much. "Well, hope springs eternal."

That remark pricked deep enough to obliterate Emma's restraint. "Shut up, Liz."

"Ooh, Touchy." Liz sounded amused. "Significant sign."

Emma couldn't deny it. She was touchy about Mason. She always had been. "I'm sorry. Habitual response. He's totally insignificant to me now," she reminded herself as much as Liz. "All that happened a long time ago."

"Evidently, not long ago enough."

Emma bristled, stuffed her free hand deeper into her black jacket's pocket. "Excuse me?"

"The wound is still wide open, Em. It's in your voice."

Was it? Probably was. She denied it anyway. "It's not."

"It is. It's evident," Liz insisted. "But let's don't waste time arguing the point. Either way, never kick an opportunity to the curb. That door is opening again for a reason."

"Yeah, right." Emma rolled her eyes back in her head, stared at the white ceiling, blanking out old memories she thought she had forgotten. "He's probably married with a couple of kids by now."

"Mmm, maybe. Want me to take a look?"

"No!" Emma cringed at having elevated her voice and then lowered it. Fortunately, others hadn't crowded into the alcove, so no one had overheard her. "No, I do not." Liz bent the odd rule when it was essential to mission success, but to violate his privacy on a personal interest? That was unexpected. So was the temptation to let Liz look. Not that Emma would give in to it.

"Okay, then." Liz sounded unaffected, as if the offer had been a test. "Well, if you change your mind…"

Definitely a test. Thankful Emma had tamped curiosity and refused, she assured Liz, "I won't."

"Fine. But if you do—"

"I won't, Liz." Emma sniffed. "Some opportunities need to be kicked to the curb and some doors are best left shut."*

THE STORMWATCH SERIES

Holly, the worst winter storm in eighty years...

Holly blows in with subzero temperatures, ice and snow better measured in feet than in inches, and leaves devastation and destruction in its wake. But, in a storm, the weather isn't the only threat—and those are the stories told in the STORMWATCH series. Track the storm through these six chilling romantic suspense novels:

FROZEN GROUND by Debra Webb, Montana
DEEP FREEZE by Vicki Hinze, Colorado
WIND CHILL by Rita Herron, Nebraska
BLACK ICE by Regan Black, South Dakota
SNOW BRIDES by Peggy Webb, Minnesota
SNOW BLIND by Cindy Gerard, Iowa

Get the Books at Amazon

ABOUT THE AUTHOR

DEBRA WEBB is the USA Today bestselling author of more than 150 novels, including reader favorites the Faces of Evil, the Colby Agency and the Shades of Death series. She is the recipient of the prestigious Romantic Times Career Achievement Award for Romantic Suspense as well as numerous Reviewers Choice Awards. In 2012 Debra was honored as the first recipient of the esteemed L. A. Banks Warrior Woman Award for her courage, strength, and grace in the face of adversity. Recently Debra was awarded the distinguished Centennial Award for having achieved publication of her 100th novel. With this award Debra joined the ranks of a handful of authors like Nora Roberts and Carole Mortimer.

With more than four million books sold in numerous languages and countries, Debra's love of storytelling goes back to her childhood when her mother bought her an old typewriter in a tag sale. Born in Alabama, Debra grew up on a farm and spent every available hour exploring the world around her and creating her stories. She wrote her first story at age nine and her first romance at thirteen. It wasn't until she spent three years working for the Commanding General of the US Army in Berlin behind the Iron Curtain and a five-year stint in NASA's Shuttle Program that she realized her true calling. A collision course between suspense and romance was set. Since then she has expanded her work into some of the darkest places the human psyche dares to go. Visit Debra at www.debrawebb.com.

ALSO BY DEBRA WEBB

Trust No One

The Darkness We Hide

Secrets and Lies

The Undertaker's Daughter
The Lies We Tell
The Secrets We Bury
The Undertaker's Daughter

The Safest Lies
A Winchester, Tennessee Thriller

When You Come Back

the dead girl
BREAKDOWN Series

For a complete listing of Debra Webb's books, visit her website at
debrawebb.com

DON'T MISS!

THE EXPLOSIVE SUSPENSE SERIES

A ground-breaking, fast paced 4-book suspense series that will keep you turning pages until the end. Reviews describe BREAKDOWN as "unique," "brilliant" and "the best series of the year." The complete series includes **the dead girl** by Debra Webb, **so many secrets** by Vicki Hinze, **all the lies** by Peggy Webb and **what she knew** by Regan Black. You'll want all four books of the thrilling BREAKDOWN series!

Printed in Great Britain
by Amazon